Simply Learning, Simply Best

Simply Learning, Simply Best

倍斯特出版事業有限公司
Best Publishing Ltd.

Basic
圖解式英文句型+作文

孟瑞秋◎著

附便利貼光碟
輕鬆寫英文自傳、講稿、作文與信件！

附便利貼光碟

自學、教學雙效英語書 同步提升翻譯寫作實力
考場寫出好成績 職場得到最佳考績

學習特色 **全面打好寫作根基！**
從【Part 1 句型篇】漸進式學習最基礎的文法、句型，搭配生活事件、人事物描述、故事情緒與信件 4 大主題，替學習者在腦中建構句型公式，並提供與主題相關的例句，提前為下筆寫英文作文打好基礎，同時注入內容元素！

學習特色 **圖像式提升寫作能力！**
跟著【Part 2 圖解應用篇】的寫作架構圖，同時使用【Part 1 句型篇】的基礎句型為作文的零件，進而延伸應用，為腦海烙印「自傳」、「英文報告的講稿」、「英文短文」和「英文商用書信」4 大常見作文類型各段落的組成元素，一次掌握句型和作文的概念和能力！

Author's Words 作者序

　　學習英文除了基礎文法外，精通「句型」是訓練聽力與口說能力的利器，「圖解寫作」能力的建立更是閱讀及寫作的關鍵。本書針對有撰寫英文自傳、報告、短文，以及信件需求的讀者而設計。內容分「句型篇」和「圖解應用篇」兩部分。

　　經由本書循序漸進的編寫，讀者可先從第一部份「句型篇」學習寫作時常用的 24 大類型文法及句型，其中編寫採用的例句都是兼具生活化及閱讀性的常見內容。除基礎例句外，本篇也提供其他相關實用且具體的句型及單字整理，而各章節後也有重點回顧和練習的設計可強化所學。

　　對文法句型有了基礎概念後，接著第二部份「圖解應用篇」的進階能力養成是不同類型範文的閱讀。內容包含求職自傳、人物描寫、短篇作文，以及各式英文書信，共計 36 篇，可謂包羅萬象，兼具實用性及知識性。此部份「圖解寫作」的編排方式更增添讀者對寫作的深刻印象。經由「寫作分析」則可精確理解學習文章的寫法及內容外，更可增進讀者寫作技巧的能力。

　　衷心期盼在本書精密巧思設計的引導下，讀者在學習英文以及提升英文閱讀及寫作能力方面將能更上一層樓。

孟瑞秋

Editor's Words 編者序

　　英文寫作能力注重持續練習，在不斷修正，以及磨鍊文筆後，內容與文字才會更加精鍊，段落之間的連貫性、邏輯性更通順。但，這樣的實力養成並不容易，國高中時期的學生，普遍都是為了應付考試，而不得不寫，學到的寫作技巧當然也很容易就忘了，如此長期積累的惡性循環下，大多數人的寫作能力，一直都無法有穩定的提升。

　　我們能夠體會國高中生要負擔的課業壓力已很沉重，在這樣的情況下，要多分配時間給英文寫作能力的累積，並不容易。而協助學生在有限的時間下，儘量掌握文法正確性、句型的多變性，進而應用在寫作上的起、承、轉、合，拿下平均以上的高分，是本書最終的目標。

　　首先我們規劃了 **Part 1 句型篇**，並搭配清晰的圖解，讓讀者對句子（也是寫作的組成要素），有基本的文法概念，其中每句型的造句，更和生活，如大自然、人事物，甚至是故事的描述做結合，有助短時間累積寫作的靈感來源，以及實用的句型。**Part 2 圖解應用篇**則是 **Part 1 句型篇**的延伸應用，著重起、承、轉、合每個段落的寫作提示，搭配圖表呈現，有助學習者快速記憶寫作的架構，並在撰寫「自傳」、「英文簡報講稿」、「英文作文」與「英文信件」時，避免掉不知如何下筆的問題。

　　寫作能力的確需要時間培養、累積，但用「對」方式學習，才能學得「好」、學得「快」，本書就是最好的讀物，讓您一次學好文法、句型和英文寫作！別忘了用本書附上的便利貼光碟，讓它馬上解決您馬上要動筆寫英文作文的需求！還能不知不覺進入英文寫作的美好世界！

編輯部　敬上

Instructions 使用說明與學習特色

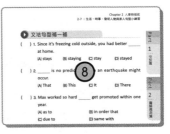

❶ 在 **Part 1 句型篇**，每個單元的重點文法以圖解的方式呈現，幫助讀者快速了解文法結構。

❷ 中英搭配的基礎例句，能夠方便了解該單元的句型內容。

❸ 『相關文法說明』有簡要、精闢的文法解說，奠定讀者對於句型文法的基礎。『其他例句』則提供更多延伸用法句型的圖解解說，以及中文翻譯，幫助讀者詳加了解更多的句型應用。

❹ 看『相關的句型』，與中英例句，搭配圖解，有效擴充讀者的句型資料庫！

❺ 除了學實用句型，還有『好用單字整理』，含單字中譯與詞性，幫助讀者掌握句型中的單字用法。

❻ 於 **Part 1 句型篇**與 **Part 2 圖解應用篇**的某些單元特規劃句型小練習，從『文法小回顧』做快速的複習，加深學習印象！

❼ 從中文翻譯和答案解析，了解學習的成果，以及不足之處。

❽ 從『文法句型補一補』的小測驗中，立即驗收所學！

❾ 看寫作老師分享寫作小技巧，為每單元的學習做完美的結尾！

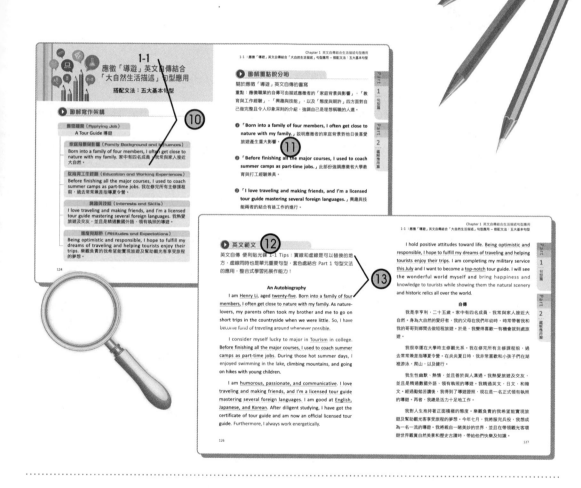

⑩ **Part 2 圖解應用篇** 每單元的依各個主題並利用圖解的方式呈現寫作的架構，幫助讀者了解該類型文章的寫法！

⑪ 『圖解重點説分明』有分析該類型的寫作原則及技巧，並有各段文章的摘要説明及寫作重點，確實印證上述的寫作方式及技巧。

⑫ 『英文範文』具體呈現各種類型的中英對照文章，提升學習效率！

⑬ 另有實線、虛線、套色部分，以清楚將 **Part 1 句型篇** 所學習到的文法句型具體標示出來，以供前後對照，並透過閱讀欣賞文章以確實應用所學！從便利貼光碟剪貼想要的文章段落，直接使用，累積寫作自信心！

References 參考書目與相關網站

Bly, Robert W., Regina Anne Kelly. *The Encyclopedia of Business Letters, Faxes, and E-Mail.* NJ: Career Press, 2009. Print.

Collins. *Skills for the TOEIC Test Speaking and Writing.* China: HarperCollins Publishers, 2012. Print.

Poe, Roy W. *The McGraw-Hill Handbook of Business Letters.* Taiwan: McGraw-Hill Education, 2006. Print.

Adams, Guy (2013)。《新世紀福爾摩斯檔案簿》（嚴麗娟譯）。台北：商周。

Corwin, Gene, Gary Joseph Grappo, and Adele Lewis. (2009)。《如何寫好英文履歷》（林錦慧、馮慧瑛譯）。台北：博識圖書。

Emmerson, Paul (2013)。《商用英文文法基礎班（雙本書）》（李盈瑩譯）。台北：寂天文化。

Hammons, Mark, David Katz, and 林建江（2014）。《外商·百大英文履歷勝經》。台北：貝塔。

LiveABC 互動英語（2013）。《CNN 全球巨星專訪 名人教你說英語》。台北：希伯崙。

LiveABC 互動英語（2016）。《CNN 主播教你用英語看懂世界趨勢》。台北：希伯崙。

LiveABC、鄭俊琪（2015）。《圖表解構英文文法》。台北：希伯崙。

Mullaney, Martin. (2001)。《腦力激盪英文作文》。台北：空中美語。

Oba, T.J.、飯泉惠美子（2006）。《用英語作簡報─初學者也 OK！》（先鋒企管出版部譯）。桃園：先鋒企管。

Taylor, Shirley (2013)。《朗文英文商業書信&電子郵件寫作技巧與範例》（林麗冠譯）。新北：台灣培生教育。

上野陽子（2014）。《賈伯斯式 職場英語力》（陸蕙貽譯）。台北：商周。

王燕希、諸葛霖（2015）。《即選即用外貿英文書信》。台北：五南。

有元美津世（2014）。《如何準備英語面試》（戴偉傑譯）。台北：眾文圖書。

沈兆鼎（2013）。《翻一次說一輩子的英文簡報速成本》。新北：知識工場。

何誠信（2006）。《最新美式自傳範本》。台北：眾文圖書。

車衡錫（2014）。《商用英文會話與 E-mail 寫作句型 233》（博碩文化、陳郁昕譯）。新北：博碩文化。

柯泰德（2007）。《有效撰寫求職英文自傳》。新北：揚智文化。

陸文玲（2016）。《空服員應試英文》。台北：眾文圖書。

陳浚德（2012）。《高中英文文法與句型全攻略》。新北：建興文化。

許寶芳、郭春安、楊毓琳、薛夙娟（2014）。《英文句型與翻譯》。高雄：晟景數位文化。

黃瑪莉（2012）。《現代商用英文》。台北：智勝文化。

楊景邁、曾淵培（2003）。《東華當代英文法—上、下冊》。台北：東華書局。

蔡章兵（2007）。《快速學會英文簡報》。新北：漢湘文化。

張翔（2015）。《打動面試官！英語口試，這樣說就過關》。新北：知識工場。

賴伯勇（2007）。《中英文自傳‧求職信‧面談英語‧履歷表‧介紹信‧推薦函範例》。台北：眾文圖書。

羅彩今（2007）。《升大學英文作文》。新北：如意文化。

趙容培、韓一（2016）。《TOEIC 多益寫作入門》（陳馨祈譯）。台北：知英文化。

鄭炎活（2015）。《英文文法拆招秘笈》。新北：龍騰文化。

鄭俊琪（2015）。《句型 x 翻譯—英語力的關鍵》。台北：希伯崙。

https://en.wikipedia.org

https://zh.wikipedia.org/zh-tw/ 中文維基百科

www.buzzle.com/articles/autobiography-essay-sample.html

www.ehow.com › Careers & Work

www.jobhero.com/resume-samples

https://templatelab.com/biography-tcmplates/ https://theessayexpert.com/samples/professional-bios

www.history.com/topics

www.biography.com/people

www.biographyonline.net/people/100-most-influential.html

www.thefamouspeople.com/profiles

http://time.com/collection/2016-time-100/

http://edition.cnn.com

http://new.time.com

http://www.charlesdickensinfo.com/christmas-carol/

http://www.livescience.com/topics/global-warming

http://www.goodletterwriting.com/

http://www.letterwritingguide.com/

http://www.businessballs.com/writing.htm

http://www.englishgrammar.org/effective-business-writing/

https://www.englishclub.com/business-english/correspondence-samples.htm

Contents 目次

2 Part 圖解應用篇

Chapter 4 | 英文信件結合英文書信用語句型應用

Part 1
句型篇

　　本部份 24 種類型的文法句型，圖解呈現的方式有助快速了解文法結構。中英對照的例句與簡要、精闢的文法解說，則可奠定句型文法的基礎；各種例句也提供延伸用法、句型的圖解解說，以及中文翻譯，可學習到更多實用且具體的句型。若能掌握並流暢使用文法句型，無論是在描寫貼近生活的景色人事物，或者是應對職場環境的信件往返，皆能運用自如，創造出極具深度的佳作。

1-1
Nature 大自然

春天時，麗莎喜歡到日本
觀賞盛開的櫻花。

**In spring, Lisa enjoys visiting Japan to
see cherry blossoms in full bloom.**

重點文法 01

・五大基本句型：

主詞	+	不及物動詞		
S		Vi		
主詞	+	及物動詞	+	受詞
S		Vt		O

▶ 關鍵技巧與例句搶先看 01

英文依及物動詞或不及物動詞的區分五種基本句型的使用

❶ 春天時，麗莎喜歡到日本觀賞盛開的櫻花。

In spring, Lisa enjoys visiting Japan to see cherry **blossoms** in full bloom.

❷ 小朋友熱愛夏天，因為刺激的夏日活動帶給他們愉快的回憶。

Children love summer because the exciting summer activities bring them pleasant **memories**.

▶ 相關文法說明

❶ 「In spring, Lisa enjoys visiting Japan to see cherry blossoms in full bloom.」此句用到基本句型 3：

★ **說明**：主詞＋及物動詞＋受詞（S + Vt + O）。及物動詞，要接受詞。enjoy 在句中接動名詞 visiting 做為受詞。

★ **其他例句**：

Willow trees around the pond	**provide**	shade and **breeze.**
S	Vt	O

環繞池塘四周的楊柳樹提供樹蔭和涼風。

❷ 「Children love summer because the exciting summer activities bring them pleasant memories.」此句用到基本句型 4：

★ **說明**：主詞＋及物動詞＋間接受詞（人）＋直接受詞（物）（S + Vt + IO + DO）。及物動詞後接兩個受詞：「間接受詞」，人，及「直接受詞」，事物者，即一般所謂的「授與動詞」。

★ **其他例句**：

The air from the cold winter time	gave	Richard	**refreshing** feelings.
S	Vt	IO	DO

寒冬的空氣給李察心神舒爽的感受。

相關的句型

除前述基本句型 3、4 外，另外有三個基本句型。

- 基本句型 1：

主詞	+	不及物動詞	+	（副詞）
S		Vi		（adv）

The warm sun **hangs** high in the blue sky on hot summer days.

炎熱夏日時，溫暖的太陽高掛藍天中。

- 基本句型 2：

主詞	+	不及物動詞	+	主詞補語
S		Vi		SC

The air at the lake **seemed** soft and **cheerful**.

湖泊的空氣似乎輕柔宜人。

- 基本句型 5：

主詞	+	及物動詞	+	受詞	+	受詞補語
S		Vt		O		OC

After the rain, we **found** beautiful **rainbows** spreading all the way across the sky.

下過雨後，我們發現美麗的彩虹橫貫天際。

▶ 好用單字整理

	單字	詞性	中譯
1.	blossom	n.	花朵；花簇
2.	memory	n.	記憶；回憶
3.	willow	n.	柳樹；柳木
4.	provide	n.	提供；供給
5.	breeze	n.	微風；和風
6.	refreshing	adj.	提神的；清涼的
7.	hang	v.	懸掛；吊掛
8.	cheerful	adj.	高興的；令人愉快的
9.	rainbow	n.	虹；彩虹
10.	spread	v.	伸展；延伸

1-2
Rural Life 鄉間生活

格林先生周末時經常前往他的鄉村
小屋享受寧靜的鄉村氣氛。

**Mr. Green usually goes to his country cottage on
weekends to enjoy the tranquil rural atmosphere.**

重點文法 02

• 動詞時態：

主詞 +	動詞
S	（am/is/are, was/were, V/-s/-es, V-ed, shall/will VR）

▶ 關鍵技巧與例句搶先看 02

了解英文中動詞時態的運用

❶ 格林先生周末時經常前往他的鄉村小屋享受寧靜的鄉村氣氛。

Mr. Green usually goes to his country **cottage** on weekends to enjoy the **tranquil** rural **atmosphere**.

❷ 凱爾擁有快樂的童年記憶，因為他在祖父的休閒農場上過著輕鬆愜意的生活。

Kyle had pleasant childhood memories by living an easy and carefree life in his grandfather's **leisure** farm.

▶ 相關文法說明

❶ 「Mr. Green usually goes to his country cottage on weekends to enjoy the tranquil rural atmosphere.」此句用到動詞時態的現在簡單式：

★ **說明**：主詞＋現在式動詞（S + am/is/are, V/-s/-es）。現在式用以表示習慣性的事情。主詞 Mr. Green 是第三人稱單數，go 字尾要加 es。

★ **其他例句**：

Living in the rural areas, we always	**breathe** fresh air, listen to happy birds chirping, and **appreciate** the crystal clear water in the stream.	
S	Vt (breath, listen to, appreciate)	O (fresh air, happy birds chirping, the crystal clear water in the stream)

居住在鄉間，我們經常呼吸新鮮空氣，聆聽快樂的鳥啁啾鳴唱，並且欣賞清澈透明的溪水。

❷ 「Kyle had pleasant childhood memories by living an easy and carefree life in his grandfather's leisure farm.」用到動詞時態的過去簡單式：

★ **說明**：主詞＋過去式動詞（S + was/were, V-ed）。過去式用以表示過去發生的事情。提及「童年記憶」，主詞 Kyle 後接過去式 had。

★ 其他例句：

Last September in Canada, we	were **impressed** by	the beautiful maple leaves in the national park.
S	Vt	O

去年九月在加拿大，我們驚豔於國家公園裡美麗的楓葉。

▶ 相關的句型

動詞時態的未來簡單式

• 表示一般未來發生的事情：

主詞	+	未來式動詞
S		shall/will VR

You **will be** surprised to feel the friendliness and **hospitality** of the country folks next time when you visit Puli.

下回去埔里遊玩時，你將會驚訝地感受到鄉下人的友善和殷勤好客。

• 表示即將發生的未來：

主詞	+	未來式動詞
S		be going to VR

It looks dark and cloudy. In no time, there **is going to be** great **thundershowers** in the mountains.

天色看起來昏暗。很快地，山區將會下大雷雨。

▶ **好用單字整理**

	單字	詞性	中譯
1.	cottage	*n.*	農舍；小屋；（度假）別墅
2.	tranquil	*adj.*	平靜的；安寧的
3.	atmosphere	*n.*	氣氛；氛圍
4.	leisure	*n.*	悠閒；休閒
5.	breathe	*v.*	呼吸；吸氣
6.	chirp	*v.*	發啁啾聲；唧唧叫
7.	appreciate	*v.*	欣賞；感激
8.	impress	*v.*	感動；印象深刻
9.	hospitality	*n.*	好客；殷勤招待
10.	thundershower	*n.*	雷陣雨；大雷雨

1-3
Street Scenes 街景

在耶誕時節，街上所有的商店美麗地
裝飾著色彩繽紛、燦爛奪目的耶誕樹。

During the Christmas season, all the stores on the streets are
beautifully decorated with colorful, twinkling Christmas trees.

重點文法 03

- 主動與被動語態：

主詞	+	動詞	+	受詞
S		Vt		O

- 另可轉換成：

主詞	+	be 動詞	+	過去分詞 (Vp.p.) + by	+	受詞
S		be V		Vp.p. + b y		O

▶ 關鍵技巧與例句搶先看 03

英文中主動與被動語態的運用

❶ 在耶誕時節，街上所有的商店美麗地裝飾著色彩繽紛、燦爛
奪目的耶誕樹。

During the Christmas season, all the stores on the streets
are beautifully **decorated** with colorful, **twinkling** Christmas
trees.

❷ 在嘉年華遊行後，整齊乾淨的街道被群眾弄得髒亂不堪。

After the **carnival** parade, the tidy and clean streets were
polluted and messed up by the crowd.

▶ 相關文法說明

❶「During the Christmas season, all the stores on the streets are beautifully decorated with colorful, twinkling Christmas trees.」此句用到現在簡單式的被動語態：

★ **說明**：主詞＋be 動詞＋過去分詞＋by＋受詞（S am/is/are + p.p. by + O）。all the stores 是複數，be 動詞＋p.p.用 are decorated。

★ **其他例句**：

With a lot of **high-rise** buildings, **gorgeous** department stores, and fancy vehicles in it, Taipei's **prosperity**	is clearly seen	by the world.
S	V (be V + p.p.)	by + O

有著許多高聳的建築、炫麗的百貨公司，以及豪華的車輛，台北的繁榮清楚地為世人所見。

❷「After the carnival parade, the tidy and clean streets were polluted and messed up by the crowd.」此句用到過去簡單式的被動語態：

★ **說明**：主詞＋be 動詞過去式＋過去分詞＋by 受詞（S was/were + p.p. by + O）。主詞 streets 複數，用 were polluted and messed up。

★ 其他例句：

Before strict **regulations**, Taipei streets	were once taken over	by large numbers of **flyers**.
S	V (be V + p.p.)	by + O

在嚴格管制前，台北街頭曾經一度充斥著大量的廣告宣傳單。

▶ **相關的句型**

下列是被動語態常用的結構句型。

● **被動語態的形式，但是具主動的意義：**

主詞	+	be 動詞	+	過去分詞	+	介系詞	+	受詞
S		Vi		p.p.		prep		O

Though not feeling well, Lucy **is** still devoted to (= still devotes herself to) making preparations for tomorrow's **exhibition** of Parisian street scenes in the art gallery.

雖然健康欠佳，露西仍舊致力於準備明天將在美術館展出巴黎街景繪畫的作品展。

● **「被視為理所當然」的句型：**

It	+	be 動詞	+	taken for granted that	+	名詞子句
S		is/was		taken for granted that		S + V

It **is** taken for granted that if you **jaywalk** on the street, you **will be** stopped by a policeman.

假使你擅闖馬路，你會被警察阻攔是件理所當然的事。

▶ 好用單字整理

	單字	詞性	中譯
1.	decorate	*v.*	裝飾；佈置
2.	twinkling	*adj.*	閃亮的；閃爍的
3.	carnival	*n.*	狂歡節；嘉年華會
4.	high-rise	*adj.*	高樓的；高聳的
5.	gorgeous	*adj.*	燦爛的；華麗的
6.	prosperity	*n.*	繁榮；興旺
7.	regulation	*n.*	規定；控制
8.	flyer	*n.*	廣告傳單
9.	exhibition	*n.*	展覽；展示會
10.	jaywalk	*v.*	（無視交通規則）亂穿馬路

▶ 相關文法說明

❶ 「Nowadays, people can use iPads instead of the Traditional TV to watch TV programs.」此句使用到情態助動詞 can：

★ **說明**：主詞＋助動詞＋原形動詞＋（受詞）（S + aux + VR + (O)）。情態助動詞 can 用以表示「能力；可能」，後接原形動詞。

★ **其他例句**：

TV	can offer	the **viewers** a lot of programs to choose from and enjoy to the full.
S	aux + VR	O

電視能夠提供許多節目供觀眾選擇並盡情享受。

❷ 「Adults shouldn't waste too much time watching TV but should exercise more for good health.」此句用到情態助動詞 should 的否定：

★ **說明**：主詞＋否定助動詞＋原形動詞＋（受詞）（S + aux not + VR + (O)）。should 用以表示「應該」，否定時加上 not。（=shouldn't）

★ **其他例句**：

Children	shouldn't watch	too many **violent** cartoons on TV or they may **imitate** what they see.
S	aux not + VR	O

兒童不應該觀看太多電視上富含暴力的卡通，否則他們可能會模仿。

▶ 相關的句型

●（過去）習慣於……

主詞	+	used to	+	原形動詞
S		used to		VR

Mrs. Bush used to make TV, along with other **technological products** like iPads, a babysitter for her **restless** child.

布希太太過去習慣於讓電視，連同其他如平板電腦的科技產品，充當照顧她好動小孩的褓姆。

● 最好……

主詞	+	had better	+	原形動詞
S		had better		VR

We had better watch **unique** educational TV programs to keep us well-informed.

我們最好觀看優質、富教育性的電視節目來增廣見聞。

▶ 好用單字整理

	單字	詞性	中譯
1.	nowadays	*adv.*	現今；目前
2.	traditional	*adj.*	傳統的；慣例的
3.	waste	*v.*	浪費；消耗
4.	viewer	*n.*	觀看者；電視觀眾
5.	violent	*adj.*	激烈的；暴力的
6.	imitate	*v.*	模仿；仿效
7.	technological	*adj.*	技術的；科技的
8.	product	*n.*	產品；產物
9.	restless	*adj.*	焦躁不安的；靜不下來的
10.	unique	*adj.*	獨特的；極好的

Part 1 句型篇

Part 2 圖解應用篇

1-5
TV Programs 電視節目

觀看 HBO 頻道的電影等同很輕鬆
舒適地在家中看票房大賣的電影。

To watch films on HBO is to watch box office hit easily and comfortably at home.

重點文法 05

・不定詞句型：

不定詞	＋	原形動詞	＋	單數動詞	＋	（受詞）
to		VR		V-s/es		O

▶ 關鍵技巧與例句搶先看 05

了解英文中不定詞的運用

❶ 觀看 HBO 頻道的電影等同很輕鬆舒適地在家中看票房大賣
的電影。

To watch films on HBO is to watch box office **hit** easily and
comfortably at home.

❷ 使用智慧型 3D 電視的互動功能非常好玩。

It's great fun to make use of the **interactive functions** of a
Smart 3D TV.

▶ 相關文法說明

❶ 「To watch films on HBO is to watch box office hit easily and comfortably at home.」此句用到不定詞作主詞的功用：

★ **說明**：不定詞＋原形動詞＋單數動詞＋（受詞）（To VR + V-s/es + (O)）。不定詞作主詞用時，後面接單數動詞。

★ 其他例句：

To purposely **exaggerate** TV commercials	always means	to successfully **boost** the sales of the products.
S (To VR)	Vt	O (to VR)

蓄意地誇大電視廣告一向意味著，可以成功地促進產品的銷售量。

❷ 「It's great fun to make use of the interactive functions of a Smart 3D TV.」此句用到虛主詞 it 取代不定詞的用法：

★ **說明**：虛主詞＋be 動詞＋形容詞＋不定詞（It + be V + adj + to VR）。不定詞放在句首做主詞用過長時，用 it 取代，不定詞放在句尾。

★ 其他例句：

It	is	necessary for the live TV newscasts of violent scenes	to be strictly **regulated**.
S	V	adj	S (to VR)

暴力場景的電視現場轉播有必要做嚴格的管控。

● ……如此地……，以致於……

主詞	+	動詞	+	so	+	形容詞	+	as to	+	原形動詞
S		V		so		O		as to		VR

The anchor is so **aggressive** as to do both the routine jobs of **covering** daily news and reporting news for the network.

這名電視主播是如此地有進取心，以致於做每日例行的採訪工作並且為電視網報導新聞。

● 獨立不定詞常置於句首、句中，或句尾，用以修飾全句。

To VR/To be	+	形容詞	+	……
To VR/To be		adj.,		……

To sum up, due to the **popularity** of Korean soap operas, fans in Taiwan have a **craze** for Korean food, fashion, language, and so on.

總而言之，由於韓劇的流行，台灣粉絲瘋狂於韓式的食物、服裝、語言等等。

▶ 好用單字整理

	單字	詞性	中譯
1.	hit	*n.*	受歡迎（賣座的）人或事物
2.	interactive	*adj.*	互動的；相互作用的
3.	function	*n.*	功能；作用
4.	exaggerate	*v.*	誇張；言過其實
5.	boost	*v.*	推動；提高
6.	regulate	*v.*	管理；控制
7.	aggressive	*adj.*	進取的；積極的
8.	cover	*v.*	採訪；報導
9.	popularity	*n.*	流行；大眾化
10.	craze	*n.*	狂熱；瘋狂（風尚）

1-6
News 新聞
透過安裝在手機的新聞應用程式
閱讀新聞是方便且即時的。
Reading news through the news Apps installed on the Smartphone is convenient and impromptu.

重點文法 06

• 動名詞句型：

動名詞	+	單數動詞	+	受詞
V.ing		V-s/es		O

▶ 關鍵技巧與例句搶先看 06

了解英文中動名詞的運用

❶ 透過安裝在手機的新聞應用程式閱讀新聞是方便且即時的。

Reading news through the news Apps **installed** on the Smartphone is convenient and **impromptu**.

❷ 今日的演藝人員習慣於利用社群網站，如臉書、推特、即時圖片分享（Instagram）等來提升知名度。

Entertainers nowadays are **accustomed** to **enhancing** their celebrity rating via social networking, such as Facebook, Twitter, Instagram, etc.

▶ 相關文法說明

❶ 「Reading news through the news Apps installed on the Smartphone is convenient and impromptu.」此句用到動名詞作主詞的功用：

★ **說明**：動名詞＋單數動詞＋（受詞）（V.ing + V-s/es + (O)）。動名詞作主詞用時，後面接單數動詞。

★ **其他例句**：

Making a correct judgment on whatever we read	protects	us from being misled by improper or **distorted** news reports.
S (V.ing)	Vt	O

無論閱讀什麼我們都能做正確的判斷，可以保護我們免於被不適當或扭曲的新聞報導所誤導。

❷ 「Entertainers nowadays are accustomed to enhancing their celebrity rating via social networking, such as Facebook, Twitter, Instagram, etc.」此句用到介系詞後接動名詞的功用：

★ **說明**：主詞＋動詞＋介系詞＋動名詞＋（受詞）（S + V + prep + V.ing + (O)）。介系詞後遇動詞時，動詞要改成動名詞做為受詞。

★ 其他例句：

We	keep us informed of **current** news events all over the world	by	visiting **international** websites.
S	Vt	prep	O (V.ing)

我們藉由瀏覽國際網站來得知全世界正在發生的新聞事件。

▶ 相關的句型

● ～不～；～不可能／無法～：

There ＋ be 動詞 ＋ no＋動名詞＋that ＋ 主詞＋動詞
There　　　　is　　　no　　V-ing　that　　S　　V

There is no surprising that Jerry was **severely** punished in class today because he was caught watching NBA news on his iPad.

傑瑞今天在課堂上遭到嚴厲處分並不令人驚訝，因為他被逮到用平板電腦看 NBA 的新聞。

● ～不用說～；～自不待言～：

It goes without ＋ 動名詞＋that ＋ 主詞＋動詞
It goes without　　saying　that　　　S　　V

It goes without saying that when reading the newspaper every day, Thomas **glances** over only the **headlines** because he is such a busy person.

不用說，湯瑪士每天閱讀報紙時，只有瀏覽標題，因為他是如此忙碌的人。

▶ 好用單字整理

	單字	詞性	中譯
1.	install	*v.*	安裝；設置
2.	impromptu	*adj.*	即席的；即時的
3.	accustom	*v.*	習慣於；適應於
4.	enhance	*v.*	提高；增加
5.	distorted	*adj.*	扭曲的；曲解的
6.	current	*adj.*	現時的；當前的
7.	international	*adj.*	國際的；國際間的
8.	glance	*v.*	瀏覽；粗略地看
9.	headline	*n.*	標題；頭版頭條新聞
10.	severely	*adv.*	嚴厲地；嚴重地

2-1
People 名人

據報導歐普拉‧溫芙蕾的電視脫口秀獲得高收視率，並且對美國的大眾文化產生很大的影響。

It is reported that Oprah Winfrey's TV talk show received a high television rating and has greatly influenced the American popular culture.

重點文法 01

・虛詞 it 的句型：

It	+	be 動詞	+	過去分詞	+	that	+	主詞＋動詞
S		be V		V-pp.		that		S　　V

・虛詞 there 的句型：

There	+	be 動詞	+	no＋動名詞
S		be V		no　　V-ing

▶ 關鍵技巧與例句搶先看 01

了解英文中虛詞 it 及 there 句型的運用

❶ 據報導歐普拉‧溫芙蕾的電視脫口秀獲得高收視率，並且對美國的大眾文化產生很大的影響。

It's reported that Oprah Winfrey's TV talk show **received** a high television rating and has greatly **influenced** the American popular culture.

❷ 牆上掛有名人用餐照片的餐廳普受歡迎是無可否認的。

There is no denying the **popularity** of a restaurant with pictures of celebrities who had eaten there on the wall.

▶ 相關文法說明

❶「It's reported that Oprah Winfrey's TV talk show received high viewing rate and has greatly influenced the American popular culture.」此句用到虛詞 it 的句型：

★ **說明**：假主詞 it 常用以取代由 that 引導名詞子句的真正主詞。**句型**：It＋be 動詞＋過去分詞＋that＋主詞＋動詞。

★ 其他例句：

It	is reported that	celebrities often	wear **disguises** when going out to avoid **paparazzi**'s picture-taking.
It	beV pp that	S	V + O

據報導，名人為了要躲避狗仔隊的拍攝，外出時經常變裝。

❷「There is no denying the popularity of a restaurant with pictures of celebrities who had eaten there on the wall.」這是虛詞 there 的句型：

★ **說明**：虛詞 there 可用以形成特定語意的句型。**句型**：虛詞 there 的句型：There＋be 動詞＋no＋動名詞＋受詞。

★ 其他例句：

There **is**	no denying	Alicia's feeling better after her coming back from the **concert** of the Korean idol singing group, CNBLUE.
There be V	no　Ving	O

艾麗西亞在欣賞過韓國偶像團體 CNBLUE 的演唱會回來後，心情好多了是無可否認的。

▶ 相關的句型

● （某人）很樂意／榮幸來……

It	+	be 動詞	+	所有格	+	pleasure/honor	+	不定詞
It		be V		one's		pleasure/honor		to V

It's my great **pleasure** to **introduce** you the Beatles, the most popular and most-loved English pop group in the 1960s.

我很樂意來為各位介紹「披頭四」，也就是在 60 年代，最受歡迎而且最為歌迷所喜愛的英國流行樂團。

● 不用～：

There	+	be 動詞	+	no＋名詞＋that	+	主詞＋動詞
There		be V		no N that		S V

In **conclusion**, there is no doubt that due to the different styles of the actors, the Korean soap operas are more attractive than the Taiwanese TV series.

最後結論是，無庸自疑地，由於演員不同的風格，韓劇較台灣連續劇吸引人。

▶ 好用單字整理

	單字	詞性	中譯
1.	receive	*v.*	得到；受到
2.	influence	*v.*	影響；起作用
3.	popularity	*n.*	受歡迎；討人喜歡
4.	disguise	*n.*	假扮；偽裝
5.	paparazzi	*n.*	狗仔隊
6.	concert	*n.*	音樂會；演唱會
7.	pleasure	*n.*	愉快；樂事
8.	introduce	*v.*	介紹；引見
9.	conclusion	*n.*	結論；結尾
10.	attractive	*adj.*	吸引的；引人注目的

2-2
People 發明家

請看這張投影片。這是 YouTube，全世界最知名的影片分享及觀看的網站。
它是在 2005 年由史蒂夫‧陳，查德‧賀利，及賈德‧卡林姆所創建的。

Look at this slide here, please. This is YouTube, the world's most popular video sharing and
viewing website. It was created by Steve Chen, Chad Hurley, and Jawed Karim in 2005.

重點文法 02

‧祈使句句型：

（主詞）	+	原形動詞	+	受詞
(You)		VR		O

▶ 關鍵技巧與例句搶先看 02

了解英文中祈使句句型的運用

❶ 請看這張投影片。這是 YouTube，全世界最知名的影片分享
及觀看的網站。它是在 2005 年由史蒂夫‧陳、查德‧賀
利，及賈德‧卡林姆所創建的。

Look at this **slide** here. This is YouTube, the world's most
popular video sharing and viewing **website**. It was created
by Steve Chen, Chad Hurley, and Jawed Karim in 2005.

❷ 善用這由希爾凡‧高曼所發明的購物車，那麼你將買齊所有
你想買的東西。

Make good use of the shopping cart **invented** by Sylvan
Goldman here, and you can buy everything you want.

▶ 相關文法說明

❶ 「Look at this slide here. This is YouTube, the world's most popular video sharing and viewing website.」此句用到祈使句句型：

★ **說明**：(You)＋原形動詞＋（受詞）。主詞 You 省略，後接原形動詞。

★ **其他例句**：

(You)	Take a look at	the slide of this man: Martin Cooper, who invented the first handheld **mobile** phone in the world in 1973.
(S)	VR	O

看看這張投影片。這是馬汀·庫柏，他在 1973 年發明了全世界第一支的手持行動電話。

❷ 「Make good use of the shopping cart invented by Sylvan Goldman here, and you can buy everything you want.」此句用到祈使句句型：

★ **說明**：(You)＋原形動詞＋（受詞），and 主詞＋動詞＋（受詞）（(You) + VR + (O), and S + V + (O)）。中文解釋為：
～，那麼～

★ 其他例句：

(You)	Try	Facebook, **developed** by Mark Zuckerberg in 2004,	and you can create a personal **profile**, make online friends, and **exchange** messages.
(S)	VR	O,	and S + V + O

試用由馬克・祖柏格在 2004 年創辦的臉書看看，那麼你就可以建立個人頁面、結交網友，以及交換留言。

▶ 相關的句型

● 讓我們～：

Let's	+	原形動詞	+	（受詞）
Let's		VR		(O)

Let's **pay** our respect to Steve Jobs, who was one of the **original** inventors of the Apple computers, the "user-friendly" computers for ordinary people.

讓我們對史蒂夫・賈伯斯致敬。他是供一般人"簡易使用"蘋果電腦的原始發明家之一。

● ～，否則～：

句型：

主詞 + 原形動詞 + (受詞),			or 主詞 + 動詞 + （受詞）		
(You)	VR	(O),	or S	V	(O)

Use the wireless 3D Wii **Remote**, or you cannot play Wii. It was the **best-selling** video game created by Nintendo in 2006. 使用無線 3D Wii 遙控器，否則你無法玩 Wii。它是在 2006 年由任天堂所創造銷售最佳的電玩。

▶ **好用單字整理**

	單字	詞性	中譯
1.	slide	*n.*	幻燈片
2.	website	*n.*	網站
3.	invent	*v.*	發明；創造
4.	mobile	*adj.*	可動的；移動式的
5.	develop	*v.*	開發；研製
6.	profile	*n.*	概述；簡介
7.	exchange	*v.*	交換；交流
8.	original	*adj.*	原始的；有獨創性的
9.	remote	*adj.*	遙遠的；遙控的
10.	best-selling	*adj.*	暢銷的；賣座的

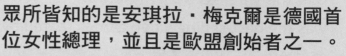

2-3
People 新聞人物

眾所皆知的是安琪拉‧梅克爾是德國首位女性總理，並且是歐盟創始者之一。

It is a well-known fact that Angela Merkel is the first female chancellor of Germany and one of the architects of the European Union.

重點文法 03

• that 名詞子句：

It	+	be 動詞	+	N/adj	+	that	+	主詞＋動詞
S		be V		N/adj		that		S V

• what 名詞子句：

What	+	主詞	+	動詞	+	be 動詞	+	that	+	主詞＋動詞
What		S		V		be V		that		S V

▶ 關鍵技巧與例句搶先看 03

了解英文中名詞子句句型的運用

❶ 眾所皆知的是安琪拉‧梅克爾是德國首位女性總理，並且是歐盟創始者之一。

It is a well-known fact that Angela Merkel is the first female **chancellor** of Germany and one of the **architects** of the European Union.

❷ 比爾‧蓋茲總是抱持著應該讓世界變得更好的理念，並且致力於從事慈善活動。

What Bill Gates always has in mind is that he should make the world a better place and he **dedicates** himself to **charitable** causes.

▶ 相關文法說明

❶「It is a well-known fact that Angela Merkel is the first female chancellor of Germany and one of the architects of the European Union.」此句用到以 it 虛主詞結合 that 名詞子句作為真主詞的句型：

★ **說明**：It＋be 動詞＋N/adj＋that＋主詞＋動詞。

★ **其他例句**：that 名詞子句也可用以引導同位語作用的子句。

Warren Buffet	is admired	for the fact that his **investment strategy** has made him one of the richest men in the world.
S	Vt	the fact + that + S +V

華倫・巴菲特極受崇拜是因為他的投資策略促使他成為全世界最富有的人之一。

❷「What Bill Gates always has in mind is that he should make the world a better place and he dedicates himself to charitable causes.」此句用到關係詞引導名詞子句作為主詞作用的句型：

★ **說明**：What＋主詞＋動詞＋be 動詞＋that＋主詞＋動詞。

★ 其他例句：

What Tadashi Yanai, the **founder** of Uniqlo, planned to do	was	that he would build a Uniqlo University to train new store managers.
What + S + V	be V	that + S +V

優衣庫的創辦人，Tadashi Yanai，計畫要建立一所優衣庫大學以訓練新任的商店經理人才。

▶ 相關的句型

名詞子句可用以當及物動詞的受詞或主詞補語。

● ～宣佈～：

主詞	+	及物動詞	+	that	+	主詞＋動詞
S		announce		that		S V

Howard Schultz, the CEO of Starbucks, once **announced** that he **resigned** from the post in 2000. However, he returned to head the company in 2008.

霍華・舒茲，星巴克的總裁，曾在 2000 年宣佈辭職。但是，他在 2008 年又重返領導公司。

● ～的原因是～：

～reason why	主詞＋動詞 + be 動詞 + that + 主詞＋動詞				
～reason why	S V	be V	that	S	V

One reason why Pope Francis is now **particularly** catching the world's attention is that he's trying to bring some changes to the church itself.

現今為何法蘭西斯教宗特別受到全世界矚目的原因，是他正試圖對教會做些改變。

▶ 好用單字整理

	單字	詞性	中譯
1.	chancellor	*n.*	大臣；總理
2.	architect	*n.*	建築師；創造者
3.	dedicate	*v.*	奉獻；致力於
4.	charitable	*adj.*	慈善的；慈善事業的
5.	investment	*n.*	投資
6.	strategy	*n.*	策略；計策
7.	founder	*n.*	創立者；建立者
8.	announce	*v.*	宣佈；聲稱
9.	resign	*v.*	辭職；辭去
10.	particularly	*adv.*	特別地；尤其

2-4
People 影響人物 1

深受 J.K.羅琳哈利波特系列的影響，艾歷克斯
認為假使他有魔法，他便可以施展各種把戲。

Deeply influenced by J. K. Rowling's Harry Potter serials, Alex thought
that if he had magic powers, he could play all kinds of tricks.

重點文法 04

假使語氣句型：

· 句型 1

If＋主詞＋were/V-ed,＋主詞		would/could/ should/might	＋	原形動詞
If	S	were/V-ed,	S	would/could/ should/might

句型中 would/could/should/might ＋ 原形動詞/VR

· 句型 2

主詞	＋	wish	＋	that	＋	主詞	＋ were/V-ed
S		wish		that		S	＋ were/V-ed

▶ 關鍵技巧與例句搶先看 04

了解英文中假使語氣句型的運用

❶ 深受 J.K.羅琳哈利波特系列的影響，艾歷克斯認為假使他有
魔法，他便可以施展各種把戲。

Deeply influenced by J. K. Rowling's Harry Potter serials, Alex
thought that if he had **magic** powers, he could play all kinds
of tricks.

❷ 湯姆克魯斯，一位受歡迎的美國演員，大大地影響及啟發他

眾多的影迷，這些影迷希望他們可像他一樣勇敢及聰明。

Tom Cruise, a popular American actor, influenced and **inspired** a lot of fans of his, who wish that they could be as brave and **intelligent** as he.

▶ 相關文法說明

❶「Deeply influenced by J. K. Rowling's Harry Potter serials, Alex thought if he had magic powers, he could play all kinds of tricks.」用 if 假設語氣。

★ 說明：if 條件句用 were 或動詞過去式，結果子句 could 加原形動詞。公式：If＋主詞＋were/V-ed，主詞＋would/could/should/might＋原形動詞。

★ 其他例句：

If the King of Pop, Michael Jackson,	didn't pass away,	his fans	could enjoy more of his **wonderful** works and **performances**.
If + S	V-ed	S	could + VR + O

假使流行樂之王，麥克傑克森，沒有過世的話，他的歌迷將可以欣賞到更多他絕妙的作品及表演。

❷「Tom Cruise, a popular American actor, influenced and inspired a lot of fans of his, who wish that they could be as brave and intelligent as he.」

★ 說明：祈願與現在事實相反時，S + wish + that 子句用 were 或過去式動詞。**句型**：主詞＋wish＋that＋主詞＋were/V-ed。

★ 其他例句：

NBA Warriors fans all admire	Thompson and Curry	and wish that they also set NBA **records** with three-pointers as they do.
S + V	O	and wish that S + V-ed + O

NBA 勇士隊球迷都很崇拜湯普森以及柯瑞，並且期許可以像他們一樣用三分球締造 NBA 紀錄。

▶ 相關的句型

• 若非～；要不是～的話（與過去事實相反）：

Without 名詞…, ＋ 主詞	＋	would/could/ should/might	have ＋ 過去分詞
Without N...,	S		have p.p.

Without Ang Lee's amazing **achievements** in movie-directing, the world could not have noticed the genius and efforts of Asian people.

若非有李安電影導演驚人的成就，世人便無法注意到亞洲人的天份及努力。

• （某人）建議～（應該）～：

主詞＋suggest＋that＋主詞＋(should)＋原形動詞……

（S + suggest + that + S (should) + VR + ...）

主詞	+	suggest	+	that	+	主詞	+	(should)	+	原形動詞
S		suggest		that		S		(should)		VR

We strongly suggest that the **youngsters** nowadays (should) take Barack Obama as a model, whose hardworking and **vision** made him the most powerful and influential person in the world.

我們強烈建議今日的年輕人應該以巴拉克‧歐巴馬做為榜樣。他的努力和遠見造就他成為全世界最具有權勢及影響力的人。

▶ 好用單字整理

	單字	詞性	中譯
1.	magic	*adj.*	巫術的；魔術的
2.	inspire	*v.*	激勵；啟發
3.	intelligent	*adj.*	聰明的；有才智的
4.	wonderful	*adj.*	極好的；精彩的
5.	performance	*n.*	演出；表演
6.	record	*n.*	記錄；記載
7.	achievement	*n.*	成就；功績
8.	genius	*n.*	天賦；才華
9.	youngster	*n.*	小孩；年輕人
10.	vision	*n.*	遠見；視野

2-5
People 影響人物 2

宮崎駿藉由結合大自然、科技,以及夢幻般的世界,
創造深度以及藝術;因此,他成為國際敬重的導演。

Hayao Miyazaki created depth and artistry by combining nature, technology,
and dreamlike worlds; therefore, he became an internationally honored director.

重點文法 05

轉承副詞句型:轉承副詞句型常用以使前後句論點連接,保
持流暢連貫。

▶ 關鍵技巧與例句搶先看 05

了解英文中轉承副詞句型的運用

❶ 宮崎駿藉由結合大自然、科技,以及夢幻般的世界,創造深
度以及藝術;因此,他成為國際敬重的導演。

Hayao Miyazaki created depth and artistry by combining
nature, **technology**, and dreamlike worlds; therefore, he
became an **internationally** honored director.

❷ 華特・迪士尼建造迪士尼樂園並非只是為了孩童。事實上,
他是為大人所建造的,期許有一個地方讓小孩和大人可以平
等地共同享受。

Walt Disney didn't create Disneyland only for children. In
fact, he did it for adults, wishing there were a place where
children and adults could together enjoy **equally**.

▶ 相關文法說明

❶「Hayao Miyazaki created depth and artistry by combining nature, technology, and dreamlike worlds; therefore, he became an internationally honored director.」therefore 是表示結果的轉承副詞。

★ **說明**：表示相反的可用 however,、whereas,、on the contrary, ……等。

★ **其他例句**：

The influential scientist, Stephen hawking	wasn't **defeated** by his disease.	On the **contrary,** he	faced it bravely and lived a full and **productive** life.
S	beV + pp	S	V + O + adv

深具影響力的科學家，史蒂芬・霍金，並未被他的疾病所擊敗。相反地，他勇敢地面對它並有著充實豐富的人生。

❷「Walt Disney didn't create Disneyland only for children. In fact, he did it for adults, wishing there were a place where children and adults could together enjoy equally.」in fact 是表示強調、附加的轉承副詞片語。

★ **說明**：表示結尾的可用 to sum up,、all in all,、in conclusion, ……等。

★ 其他例句：

To sum up, when I have problems,	I will call my best friend, Bill,	who is always happy to help others.
when + S + V + O	S will V + O	who + be V + adj

總而言之，當我遇到困難的時候，我會打給我那位總是樂於助人最要好的朋友，比爾。

▶ 相關的句型

● 一為～；另一則為～：

表示並列對比的句型如下：

One～,	the other～

Leonardo da Vinci is best known for two of his **artistic** paintings. One is *Mona Lisa*, and the other is The *Last Super*, both of which **remain** among the world's most famous and admired masterpieces.

李奧納多‧達文西以他的兩幅藝術畫作世界知名。一幅是《蒙娜麗莎》，另一幅是《最後的晚餐》。這兩幅畫一直是他全世界最知名且為人仰慕的傑作。

● 第一點／首先～、第二點／其次～，……、最後一點～……：

表示次序的轉承副詞可用 firstly、next、in the first place、to begin with、secondly、thirdly、fourthly、finally、last、last but not least, ……等。

We admire Mr. King for three reasons. To begin with, he is **easygoing** and considerate. Secondly, he makes math interesting and easy to learn. Last but not least, he is always eager to share his amazing life **experiences** with us. No wonder we find him the most admirable teacher.

我們因為三個理由而崇拜金老師。首先，他平易近人且善解人意。其次，他令數學學習既有趣又簡單。最後，他總是熱情地和我們分享他驚人的生活經歷。難怪他成為我們最崇拜的老師。

▶ 好用單字整理

	單字	詞性	中譯
1.	technology	*n.*	科技；技術
2.	internationally	*adv.*	國際性地；在國際間
3.	equally	*adv.*	公平地；平等地
4.	defeat	*v.*	擊敗；戰勝
5.	contrary	*n.*	相反；對立
6.	productive	*adj.*	豐富的；有收穫的
7.	artistic	*adj.*	藝術的；美術的
8.	remain	*v.*	保持；仍是
9.	easygoing	*adj.*	脾氣隨和的；平易近人的
10.	experience	*n.*	經驗；經歷

2-6
People 家人

在美國，孩子到了 18 歲或上大學
便搬出父母的房子並非不尋常的。

In America, it is not uncommon for children to move out of
their parents' house when they turn 18 or go to university.

重點文法 06

連接詞句型：英文對等連接詞連接兩個對等子句，附屬連接
詞則連接主要子句與附屬子句。

▶ 關鍵技巧與例句搶先看 06

了解英文中連接詞句型的運用

❶ 在美國，孩子到了 18 歲或上大學便搬出父母的房子並非不
尋常的。

In America, it is not **uncommon** for children to move out of
their parents' house when they turn 18 or go to **university**.

❷ 我的家人住在市區的公寓中，而我的祖父母和其他親戚住在
郊區一棟大房子裡。

My family live in a **condo** downtown, while my grandparents
live in a big house with other relatives at the **suburbs**.

58

1-4
Good and Bad of TV 電視的優缺點

在今日，人們可以使用平板電腦取代傳統電視機來觀賞電視節目。

Nowadays, people can use iPads instead of the traditional TV to watch TV programs.

重點文法 04

・助動詞句型：

主詞	+	助動詞	+	原型動詞	+	受詞
S		aux		VR		O

▶ 關鍵技巧與例句搶先看 04

了解英文中情態助動詞的用法

❶ 在今日，人們可以使用平板電腦取代傳統電視機來觀賞電視節目。

Nowadays, people can use iPads instead of the **traditional** TV to watch TV programs.

❷ 成年人不該浪費太多時間看電視，而應該為健康著想多多運動。

Adults shouldn't **waste** too much time watching TV but should exercise more for good health.

▶ 相關文法說明

❶ 「In America, it is not uncommon for children to move out of their parents' house when they turn 18 or go to university.」 when 表示時間。

★ **說明**：其他表示時間的附屬連接詞有 as、while、before、after、until、since、as soon as, …, ……等。

★ **其他例句**：whenever 相當於 no matter when，有加強語氣作用。

My father	is	good-tempered and **humorous**.	In addition, whenever there is a holiday, he takes us out for an exciting **outing** in the countryside.
S	beV	adj	whenever + S + V + O

我的父親脾氣溫和而且幽默。此外，每當假日來臨時，他會帶我們到鄉間開心地出遊。

❷ 「My family live in a condo downtown, while my grandparents live in a big house with other relatives at the suburbs.」while 表示相反語意。

★ **說明**：其他表示相反語意的連接詞有 but 及 whereas。

★ **其他例句**：even if 表示「縱使」，because 表示「因為」。

In presence of my grandparents, my mom	never gave me a hard time	even if I did something wrong because they would always **defend** me.
S	V + O	even if/because + S + V

在我的祖父母面前，縱使我做錯事，媽媽也不會讓我難堪，因為祖父母總是會為我說話。

▶ 相關的句型

● 雖然……：

形容詞／副詞／名詞＋as/though＋主詞＋動詞＋...,＋主詞＋動詞				
Adj/Adv/N	as/though	S	V	S	V

Disappointed and angry as my mother was, she would still keep her voice down whenever we two had a serious **conflict** with each other.

雖然我的媽媽既失望又憤怒，但是每當我們有嚴重衝突時，她會保持音量降低。

● 一～就～：

No sooner had ＋ 主詞 ＋ 過去分詞＋than ＋ 主詞＋動詞				
No sooner had	S	p.p.	than	S	V-ed

No sooner had we reached the park than we started barbecuing and enjoyed the family **reunion**.

我們一到公園便開始烤肉並享受家族聚餐。

▶ 好用單字整理

	單字	詞性	中譯
1.	uncommon	*adj.*	不尋常的；罕見的
2.	university	*n.*	大學；高等學府
3.	condo	*n.*	公寓；公寓住房
4.	suburb	*n.*	郊區；城外
5.	humorous	*adj.*	幽默的；詼諧的
6.	outing	*n.*	郊遊；短途旅遊
7.	defend	*v.*	保衛；辯解
8.	disappointed	*adj.*	失望的；沮喪的
9.	conflict	*n.*	衝突；爭執
10.	reunion	*n.*	團聚；聚會

2-7

生活、時事、發明人物與家人
句型小練習

　　紮實的文法句型基礎有助於英文的學習，仔細瞭解熟悉句型語法固然花時間，但是日積月累，自然大有進步。在研究句型時，應先讀英文例句，感受語感。其次，搭配中文翻譯，確實瞭解含意。再看句型解析處，強化文法句型的認知。將文法句型整體瞭解並活用，即可增進英文實力。

▶ 文法句型補一補

(   ) 1. Since it's freezing cold outside, you had better _____ at home.

     (A) stays   (B) staying   (C) stay   (D) stayed

(   ) 2. _____ is no predicting when an earthquake might occur.

     (A) That   (B) This   (C) It   (D) There

(   ) 3. Max worked so hard _____ get promoted within one year.

     (A) as to   (B) in order that

     (C) due to   (D) same with

(   ) 4. Let's _____ started to the MRT station, or we might be late.

     (A) got   (B) get   (C) gets   (D) getting

(   ) 5. _____ is my honor to introduce our speaker today, Mr. Baker.

     (A) There   (B) It   (C) That   (D) One

(   ) 6. The reason _____ Richard was absent today was that he overslept this morning.

     (A) what   (B) for   (C) why   (D) how

▶ 答案與解析

1. (C) stay

題目中譯 由於外頭非常寒冷,你最好待在家裡。

答案解析 had better 是助動詞片語的一種,後面必須搭配原形動詞,故應選 (C) stay。

2. (D) There

題目中譯 地震何時可能發生是無從預測的。

答案解析 There is no V-ing …是使用動名詞的固定句型。故應選 (D) There。

3. (A) as to

題目中譯 麥克斯工作如此地努力以至於一年之內就升官了。

答案解析 so... as to 表示「如此地……以至於……」,不定詞 to 用以表示「結果」的固定句型,故應選 (A) as to。

4. (B) get

題目中譯 讓我們開始前往捷運車站,否則我們可能會遲到。

答案解析 Let's 表示「讓我們……」,後面必須搭配原形動詞。故選 (B) get。

5. (B) It

題目中譯 我很榮幸介紹我們今日的演講者,貝克先生。

答案解析 It is～to + VR～ 是 it 假主詞取代真主詞 to 不定詞片語的固定句型。故應選 (B) It。

6. (C) Why

題目中譯 今天李察查缺席的原因是早上他睡過頭了。

答案解析 The reason 後要搭配疑問詞 why，後接子句成為名詞子句，充當整句的主詞。故應選 (C) why。

▶ 寫作老師巧巧說

　　在英文寫作時，文法句型的應用要正確合宜，錯誤的文法句型，會使文章錯誤百出，難以瞭解。文法句型若使用得當，確實精準，便能締造佳作，文章正確無誤，內容有物，自然是篇可讀性高的好文章。

3-1
Emotions 喜、怒故事 1
所有的觀眾因為機智過人而且幽默詼諧的演講者哄堂大笑。

The audience were all roaring with laughter because of the witty and humorous speaker.

重點文法 01

• 現在分詞句型：

主詞	+	be 動詞	+	現在分詞	+	介系詞	+	名詞
S		be V		V.ing		prep		n

• 過去分詞句型：

主詞	+	be 動詞	+	過去分詞	+	介系詞	+	名詞
S		be V		pp		prep		n

▶ 關鍵技巧與例句搶先看 01

了解英文中現在分詞與過去分詞句型的運用

❶ 所有的觀眾因為機智過人而且幽默詼諧的演講者哄堂大笑。

The **audience** were all **roaring** with laughter because of the witty and humorous speaker.

❷ 這名憤怒的顧客不滿意於飯店所提供的服務。

The angry customer was **dissatisfied** with the service offered by the hotel.

▶ 相關文法說明

❶「The audience were all roaring with laughter because of the witty and humorous speaker.」此句用到現在分詞的句型：

★ **說明**：現在分詞和 be 動詞連用，可形成現在進行式。句型公式：主詞 (S)＋be 動詞 (beV)＋現在分詞 (v.ing)＋介詞 (prep)＋名詞 (n)

★ **其他例句**：現在分詞也可以有形容詞的作用，修飾名詞，表示主動含意。

All of us	found	Larry	an **annoying** roommate on account of his **eccentric** living **habits**.
S	V	O	art + v.ing + n

大家由於賴瑞古怪的生活習慣，而覺得他是一名惹人厭的室友。

❷「The angry customer was dissatisfied with the service offered by the hotel.」此句用到過去分詞的句型：

★ **說明**：過去分詞和 be 動詞連用，可形成被動語態或表達情緒感受。句型公式：主詞 (S)＋動詞 (V)＋過去分詞 (pp)＋介系詞 (prep)＋名詞 (n)

★ **其他例句**：過去分詞也可以有形容詞的作用，修飾名詞，表示被動含意。

Those	who are **content**	are **blessed** and happy.
S	who + be V + adj	be v + pp + and + adj

知足常樂。

▶ 相關的句型

- （某人）邊～邊～：

特定動詞，如 go, lie, run, sit, come, walk, stand 等完全不及物動詞，後面可接現在分詞或過去分詞，充當主詞補語的功用：

主詞	+	不及物動詞	+	現在分詞
S		Vt		V.ing

The little girl **ran** to her mother crying sadly.
小女孩傷心地哭著跑向媽媽。

- 形容詞可與現在分詞或過去分詞合併成「複合形容詞」，具有形容詞的作用，中間要加上連字號「-」。如：handsome-looking (adj-v.ing)、delicious-tasting (adj-v.ing)、odd-smelling (adj-v.ing)、red-colored (adj-pp)、purple-painted (adj-pp) 等。

It's a **time-proven** fact that a good-looking person with a **constant** smile can easily get jobs.
外表長得好看而且時常面帶微笑的人易於求職是一個不變的真理。

▶ 好用單字整理

	單字	詞性	中譯
1.	audience	*n.*	聽眾；觀眾
2.	roar	*v.*	吼叫；放聲大笑
3.	dissatisfied	*adj.*	不高興的；不滿意的
4.	annoying	*adj.*	討厭的；惱人的
5.	eccentric	*adj.*	古怪的；異乎尋常的
6.	habit	*n.*	習慣；習性
7.	content	*adj.*	滿足的；滿意的
8.	blessed	*adj.*	受祝福的；快樂的
9.	time-proven	*adj.*	經時間證明的
10.	constant	*adj.*	不變的；持續的

3-2
Emotions 喜、怒故事 2

了解到健康是成功和快樂的基礎，
約翰將自身的健康管理做得很好。

Realizing that health is the foundation of success and happiness, John does health management well.

重點文法 02

· 分詞構句句型：

現在分詞／過去分詞,	+	主詞＋動詞	
V.ing/pp,		S	V

▶ 關鍵技巧與例句搶先看 02

了解英文中分詞構句句型的運用

❶ 了解到健康是成功和快樂的基礎，約翰將自身的健康管理做得很好。

Realizing that health is the **foundation** of success and happiness, John does health **management** well.

❷ 在大城市裡迷路的陌生人焦慮地四處徘徊，最後轉向警方請求援助。

Lost in the big city, the stranger **wandered** around **anxiously** and finally turned to the police for help.

▶ 相關文法說明

❶ 「Realizing that health is the foundation of success and happiness, John does health management well.」此句用到現在分詞構句的句型：

★ **說明**：分詞構句是由對等子句或副詞子句簡化而來的結構。現在分詞表示主動意味。現在分詞構句的句型：現在分詞 (v.ing)～，主詞 (S)＋動詞 (V)

★ **其他例句**：

Feeling desperate,	the criminal	abandoned his weapon	and gave in.
v.ing + adj	S	Vt + O	and + Vi + prep

感到絕望的情況下，這名罪犯棄械投降。

❷ 「Lost in the big city, the stranger wandered around anxiously and finally turned to the police for help.」此句用到過去分詞構句的句型：

★ **說明**：分詞構句是由對等子句或副詞子句簡化而來的結構。過去分詞表示被動含意。過去分詞構句的句型：過去分詞 (pp)～，主詞 (S)＋動詞 (V)

★ **其他例句**：

Overwhelmed with great joy,	Tina's family	felt proud of her winning the gold medal in the Olymic Games.
pp + prep + O	S	Vi + adj + prep + O

Part **1** 句型篇

Part **2** 圖解應用篇

內心充滿喜悅，汀娜的家人對於她在奧運中贏得金牌感到十分地驕傲。

▶ 相關的句型

- 在分詞前加上 **not** 或 **never**，可形成否定的分詞構句：

Not/Never	+	現在分詞／過去分詞,	主詞	+	動詞
Not/Never		v.ing /pp.,	S		V

Not having any clue about the secret, the **furious** father blew his top for being kept in the dark.

對於這個祕密一無所悉，這名憤怒的父親因為被蒙在鼓裡而暴跳如雷。

- 若前後主詞不同時，保留原主詞可形成「獨立分詞構句」。**With** ＋獨立分詞構句的句型：

With	+	名詞	+	現在分詞／過去分詞,	主詞	+	動詞
With		N		v.ing/pp.,	S		V

With his cute grandson seated beside him, the lonely old man felt more **relieved** and cheerful.

有著可愛的孫子陪坐在旁，寂寞的老先生感到比較自在愉悅。

▶ 好用單字整理

	單字	詞性	中譯
1.	foundation	*n.*	建立；基礎
2.	management	*n.*	管理；處理
3.	wander	*v.*	閒逛；徘徊
4.	anxiously	*adv.*	焦急地；擔憂地
5.	desperate	*adj.*	危急的；絕望的
6.	criminal	*n.*	罪犯
7.	abandon	*v.*	遺棄；放棄
8.	overwhelmed	*adj.*	充滿感情的；壓倒的
9.	furious	*adj.*	憤怒的；猛烈的
10.	relieved	*adj.*	寬慰的；放心的

3-3
Emotions 喜、怒故事 3

剛新婚的這對夫婦開心地前往
峇里島享受新婚蜜月。

**The couple who just got married joyfully
headed for Bali to enjoy their honeymoon.**

重點文法 03

・關係子句句型：

先行詞	+	(,) who/which	+	動詞
Antecedent		(,) who/which		V

▶ 關鍵技巧與例句搶先看 03

了解英文中關係子句句型的運用

❶ 剛新婚的這對夫婦開心地前往峇里島享受新婚蜜月。

The couple who just got married **joyfully** headed for Bali to enjoy their honeymoon.

❷ 漢克是一個樂觀的人,他總是以平常心對待人生的喜悅和傷痛。

Hank is an **optimistic** person, who can always **equally** take the joys and sorrows of life well.

▶ 相關文法說明

❶ 「The couple who just got married joyfully headed for Bali to enjoy their honeymoon.」此句用到限定關係子句的句型：

★ **說明**：關係子句的先行詞用形容詞子句修飾，前面不加逗點，即為限定用法的關係子句，先行詞是人用 who，先行詞是事物則用 which。限定關係子句的句型：先行詞＋who/which＋動詞 (V)。

★ **其他例句**：

The **universal language**	which	**prevails** over the world	is the smile.
antecedent	which	V	be V + SC

全世界共通的語言是微笑。

❷ 「Hank is an optimistic person, who can always equally take the joys and sorrows of life well.」此句用到非限定關係子句的句型：

★ **說明**：關係子句的先行詞用形容詞子句修飾，前面有加逗點，即為非限定用法的關係子句，先行詞是人用 who，先行詞是事物用 which。限定關係子句的句型：先行詞＋, who/which＋動詞 (V)

★ **其他例句**：非限定用法的關係子句也可用以修飾前面整個子句。

Richard was late for the meeting again	, which	made his boss **extremely** angry.
S + be V + SC	, which	V + O + OC

理查開會再度遲到，這使得他的老闆非常地生氣。

▶ **相關的句型**

- 關係詞 how、why、when、where 等可引導關係子句，充當形容詞子句，説明方式、理由、時間、地點等，也可有名詞子句的功用，充當主詞補語或受詞補語：

主詞	+	動詞	+	be 動詞	+	how	+	主詞	+	動詞
S		V		be V		how		S		V

Moving around in the park catching *Pokémon* is how Oscar **amuses** himself now.
在公園裡到處走動捕捉寶可夢是現在奧斯卡讓自己開心的方法。

- 由 wh-疑問詞所引導的名詞子句中，what 結合了先行詞和關係代名詞，可引導名詞子句當主詞或受詞使用：

What	+	主詞	+	動詞	+	be 動詞	+	to	+	原形動詞
What		S		V		be V		to		VR

What Nancy can do to **ease** her anger and **stress** is to exercise and listen to music .
南西能夠紓緩自己憤怒和壓力的方法是做運動和聽音樂。

▶ 好用單字整理

	單字	詞性	中譯
1.	joyfully	*adv.*	喜悅地；高興地
2.	optimistic	*adj.*	樂觀的；抱樂觀看法的
3.	equally	*adv.*	相同地；平均地
4.	universal	*adj.*	一般普遍的；全世界的
5.	language	*n.*	語言；語言文字
6.	prevail	*v.*	流行；普遍存在
7.	extremely	*adv.*	極端地；非常地
8.	amuse	*v.*	取悅；消遣
9.	ease	*v.*	緩和；使舒適
10.	stress	*n.*	壓力；緊張

3-4
Emotions 哀、樂故事 1
今晚餐廳裡的客人比以往多，
氣氛越來越歡樂了。

With more guests in the restaurant than usual
tonight, the atmosphere got merrier and merrier.

重點文法 04

- 比較級句型：

主詞 + 動詞 + 形容詞～er/more+形容詞 than + 主詞
S　　V　　　　adj.～er/more adj. than　　　　S

- 最高級句型：

主詞+動詞+定冠詞+形容詞～est / most+形容詞+介系詞+名詞
S　V　the　adj～ est/ most　adj　of / in　n

▶ 關鍵技巧與例句搶先看 04

了解英文中比較級與最高級句型的運用

❶ 今晚餐廳裡的客人比以往多，氣氛越來越歡樂了。

With more guests in the **restaurant** than usual tonight, the atmosphere got **merrier** and merrier.

❷ 對凱文來說，在新年前夕失業是全世界最悲慘的事了。

To Kevin, losing his job on New Year's Eve was the most **disastrous** thing in the world.

▶ 相關文法說明

❶ 「With more guests in the restaurant than usual tonight, the atmosphere got merrier and merrier.」此句用到比較級的句型：

★ **說明**：使用比較級形容詞比較時，單音節字字尾加 er，字尾若是子音＋y，需去掉 y，加 iest。多音節字時是 more＋形容詞原級。**句型**：主詞 (S)＋動詞 (V)＋形容詞 ～er/more＋形容詞＋than…

★ **其他例句**：

The poor with **spiritual** riches	are much happier	than the rich **without**.
S	be V + adj-er	than + S

擁有充實心靈的窮人遠比欠缺心靈財富的富人快樂。

❷ 「To Kevin, losing his job on New Year's Eve was the most disastrous thing in the world.」此句用到最高級的句型：

★ **說明**：使用最高級形容詞比較時，加定冠詞 the 後接最高級，加 of 或 in 加某一範圍。單音節字字尾加 est，多音節是 most＋形容詞原級。公式：主詞 (S)＋動詞 (V)＋the＋形容詞～est/most＋形容詞＋of/in＋名詞

★ 其他例句：

A cheerful person	is most likely to make a **success** of his own life	and also **creates** the brightest life	for people around him.
S	be V + most + likely	V + the adj-est	for + n

一個愉悅的人極有可能為自己的人生帶來成功，並且為周遭的人們創造蓬勃的生氣。

▶ 相關的句型

● ～越～，～越～：表示「比例」的比較：

The	+	比較級...,	+	the	+	比較級....
The		adj/adv-er ...,		the		adj/adv-er ....

The slower the Internet **connection** got, the less patient Chris became.

電腦網路連線越慢，克里斯就變得越不耐煩。

● 前者（不）如後者一樣～：表示「同等」的比較：

主詞 1	+	動詞	+	(not) as	+	形容詞／副詞	+	as	+	主詞 2
S1		V		(not) as		adj/adv		as		S2

Winning the first prize in the science **competition** made Sam and his teammates feel as happy as **crickets**.

在科學競賽中獲得第一名使得山姆和他的隊友快樂似神仙。

▶ 好用單字整理

	單字	詞性	中譯
1.	restaurant	*n.*	餐廳；飯店
2.	merry	*adj.*	歡樂的；愉快的
3.	disastrous	*adj.*	災害的；悲慘的
4.	spiritual	*adj.*	精神上的；心靈的
5.	without	*prep.*	沒有
6.	success	*n.*	成功；勝利
7.	create	*v.*	創造；產生
8.	connection	*n.*	連接；連線
9.	competition	*n.*	競賽；競爭
10.	cricket	*n.*	蟋蟀

3-5
Emotions 哀、樂故事 2
波特一完成馬拉松賽跑後就發現自己雖然很疲倦，但是心情很好。

Hardly had Potter completed the marathon when he found himself in a good mood, though tired out.

重點文法 05

· 倒裝句句型：

副詞 ＋	助動詞 ＋	主詞 ＋	原形動詞 ＋	（受詞）
adv	aux	S	VR	(O)

▶ 關鍵技巧與例句搶先看 05

了解英文中倒裝句句型的運用

❶ 波特一完成馬拉松賽跑後就發現自己雖然很疲倦，但是心情很好。

Hardly had Potter **completed** the marathon when he found himself in a good mood, though tired out.

❷ 潘蜜拉再也不會買那個名牌的手機了，因為她對於那款手機在使用上的問題感到受挫。

No longer will Pamela buy the famous brand **smartphone**, for she was **depressed** by its usage problems.

▶ 相關文法說明

❶「Hardly had Potter completed the marathon when he found himself in a good mood, though tired out.」此句用到倒裝句的句型：

★ **說明**：否定副詞 no、not、little、never、seldom、hardly、rarely、scarcely……等，可置於句首，後接倒裝句構，以加強語氣。**句型**：副詞 (adv)＋助動詞 (aux)＋主詞 (S)＋原形動詞 (VR)

★ **其他例句**：副詞 only 也可用於倒裝結構，有加強語氣的作用。

Only when you cleverly avoid being **misunderstood** by others	can	you	stop feeling hurt and **sorrowful**.
Only + when + S + V	aux	S	VR + O

唯有聰明地避免被他人誤解，你才不會再感到受傷和難過。

❷「No longer will Pamela buy the famous brand smartphone, for she was depressed by its usage problems.」此句用到倒裝句的句型：

★ **說明**：否定副詞片語 no longer, not a word, not until, …等，亦可置於句首，後接倒裝句構，以加強語氣。**句型**：副詞 (adv)＋助動詞 (aux)＋主詞 (S)＋原形動詞 (VR)

★ 其他例句：

Not until Simon rode on the **rollercoaster**	did	he realize the fun of visiting the **amusement** park.
Not until + S + V	aux	S + VR + O

賽門直到玩雲霄飛車後才體會到去遊樂園遊玩的樂趣。

▶ 相關的句型

● ～是如此～的～，以至於……：

Such a/an＋主詞補語＋名詞＋be 動詞＋主詞 that						主詞＋動詞	
Such a/an	SC	n	be V	S	that	S	V

Such an unlucky day was today that Jason kept getting into trouble, which made him upset and **discouraged**.

今天是如此倒楣的一天以至於傑森不停地惹上麻煩，這使得他感到懊惱和灰心。

● 在任何情境之下，～也不應該～：

Under no circumstances	助動詞 ＋ 主詞 ＋ 原形動詞…, or			主詞＋動詞	
Under no circumstances	aux	S	VR ......, or	S	V

Under no **circumstances** should Vincent break his **promise** again, or he may make his girlfriend heart-broken.

文森絕對不可以再違背諾言了，否則他的女友會很傷心。

Part 1 句型篇
Part 2 圖解應用篇

▶ **好用單字整理**

	單字	詞性	中譯
1.	complete	*v.*	完成；結束
2.	smartphone	*n.*	智慧型手機
3.	depressed	*adj.*	沮喪的；憂鬱的
4.	misunderstood	*adj.*	被誤解的
5.	sorrowful	*adj.*	悲傷的；令人傷心的
6.	rollercoaster	*n.*	（娛樂設備）雲霄飛車
7.	amusement	*n.*	懸掛；吊掛
8.	discouraged	*adj.*	灰心的；氣餒的
9.	circumstance	*n.*	情況；情勢
10.	promise	*n.*	承諾；諾言

3-6
Emotions 哀、樂故事 3

上星期發生的地震不僅對人類財產造成重大的損失，也引起人們極大的恐慌。

The earthquake occurred last week not only caused huge damage to human property but aroused great panic among people.

重點文法 06

・對等與平行結構句型：

主詞 +	動詞 +	not only +	名詞 +	but (also) +	名詞
S	V	not only	N	but (also)	N

▶ 關鍵技巧與例句搶先看 06

了解英文中對等與平行結構句型的運用

❶ 上星期發生的地震不僅對人類財產造成重大的損失，也引起人們極大的恐慌。

The earthquake **occurred** last week not only caused huge damage to human **property** but **aroused** great panic among people.

❷ 年輕人既不該吃太多速食也不該喝太多含糖飲料，否則他們將面臨極嚴重的健康問題。

Young people should neither eat too much fast food nor drink too much sugary **beverages**, or they might face disastrous health problems.

▶ 相關文法說明

❶ 「The earthquake occurred last week not only caused huge damage to human property but aroused great panic among people.」

★ **說明：**此句用到對等與平行結構的句型。對等連接詞句構要連接兩個對稱結構，如兩個對等的名詞、動詞、形容詞、副詞、或片語等，不可隨意搭配。**句型：**主詞 (S)＋動詞 (V)＋not only＋名詞 (N)＋but also＋名詞 (N)

★ **其他例句：**

Hearing the bad news, Annie	not only locked herself in the room	but **wept** sadly.
S	not only + V	but (also) + V

聽到這個壞消息，安妮不僅把自己鎖在房間內並且悲傷地啜泣。

❷ 「Young people should neither eat too much fast food nor drink sugary beverages, or they might face disastrous health problems.」

★ **說明：**此句亦同，對等連接詞句構要連接兩個對稱結構，如對等的名詞、動詞等。**句型：**主詞 (S)＋neither＋動詞 (V)＋受詞 (O)＋nor＋動詞 (V)＋受詞 (O)

★ **其他例句：**either... or ...也屬於對等與平行結構句型的片語。

It's a great joy to Mona if she can	either go shopping	or go to the movies with her friends on **holidays**.
S	either + V	or + V

對蒙娜來說，假日時能夠跟朋友逛街或是看電影都是一大享受。

▶ 相關的句型

對等與平行結構常見的句型如下：

- 「不是因為……，而是因為……」為平行對等句型：

主詞＋be動詞＋not because ＋主詞		be 動詞 but because＋主詞＋動詞	
S be V	not because	S be V but because	S V

Don't take money too **seriously**. It's not because money isn't important but because money cannot buy happiness.

不要太看重金錢。原因不是因為金錢不重要，而是因為金錢買不到幸福。

- 「寧願……，而不願……」的句型，來說明平行對等的情境：

主詞 ＋ prefer to ＋ 原形動詞 ＋			rather than ＋	原形動詞
S	prefer to	VR		VR

Mrs. Miller **preferred** to joyfully **travel** around the world rather than just stay home and do the **boring** housework.

米勒太太寧願歡樂地環遊世界，而不願只是待在家裡做無聊的家事。

▶ 好用單字整理

	單字	詞性	中譯
1.	occur	*v.*	發生；出現
2.	property	*n.*	財產；資產
3.	arouse	*v.*	激起；引起
4.	beverage	*n.*	飲料
5.	weep	*v.*	哭泣；流淚
6.	holiday	*n.*	節日；假日
7.	seriously	*adv.*	嚴肅地；認真地
8.	prefer	*v.*	寧願；更喜歡
9.	travel	*v.*	旅行；遊歷
10.	boring	*adj.*	無聊的；乏味的

3-7

故事、情緒描述句型小練習

▶ 故事、情緒描述句型小回顧

　　文法句型主要可依結構、詞性、功能等類型有變化。譬如英文句子的五大句型便可變化出各種不同的結構。依英文各種不同的詞類，文法及句型也多所變化。表示各種作用的句型更是閱讀及寫作時非常實用的基礎，有助於文意的瞭解及表達。仔細熟悉活用句型語法，閱讀、造句、翻譯、寫作自然無往不利。

▶ 文法句型補一補

( ) 1. _____ knowing where to go, Nancy burst into tears.

    (A) Not   (B) Yes   (C) No   (D) Less

( ) 2. Only when one loses heath _____ he know the importance of it.

    (A) has   (B) are   (C) does   (D) ought

( ) 3. Fanny is the _____ among all the girl students in class.

    (A) pretty   (B) prettiest

    (C) prettier   (D) less pretty

( ) 4. Little Henry stood there _____; he wanted to get some candy.

    (A) cry   (B) cries   (C) crying   (D) to cry

( ) 5. Our team finally won the championship owing to not only the efforts _____ the team spirits.

    (A) or   (B) neither   (C) also   (D) but

( ) 6. The kids are visiting Disneyland tomorrow, _____ makes them extremely excited.

    (A) which   (B) where   (C) who   (D) that

Part 1 句型篇

Part 2 圖解應用篇

▶ 答案與解析

1. (A) Not

題目中譯 不知道該往哪裡走，南西突然掉眼淚。

答案解析 在「分詞構句」結構中，分詞前加上 not 或 never，即形成否定意義的分詞構句，故應選 (A) Not。

2. (C) does

題目中譯 一個人唯有在失去健康的時候才知道健康的重要。

答案解析 副詞 only 置於句首，後接倒裝句構，有加強語氣的作用。主詞 he 與動詞 know 應搭配助動詞 does，故應選 (C) does。

3. (B) prettiest

題目中譯 芬妮是班上所有女學生中最漂亮的。

答案解析 最高級比較時，形容詞字尾若是子音＋y，需去掉 y，加 iest。故應選 (B) prettiest。

4. (C) crying

題目中譯 小亨利站在那裡嚎啕大哭；他想要糖果吃。

答案解析 完全不及物動詞 stand，後面接表示主動的現在分詞，有充當主詞補語的功用。故選 (C) crying。

5. (D) but

題目中譯 我們隊終於獲得冠軍，不僅是因為我們的努力，更由於我們的團隊精神。

答案解析 對等連接詞句構連接兩個對稱結構，not only ... but …是固定的連接詞片語。故應選 (D) but。

6. (A) which

題目中譯 小朋友們明天要去迪士尼樂園玩，這使得他們感到極度地興奮。

答案解析 關係子句，前面有加逗點，即為非限定用法的關係子句，先行詞是事物用 which。故應選 (A) which。

▶ 寫作老師巧巧說

在英文故事、情緒描述句型寫作時，文法句型如**現在與過去分詞構句、比較級與最高級、關係子句、倒裝句、對等與平行結構句型等非常實用，可具體敘述故事情節**。透過精準文法句型傳達描述，各種喜、怒、哀、樂情緒交錯文章中時，便可成功創造出活躍又生動的佳作。

4-1
Letters 英文信件 1：求職信用語
由於您的徵人啟事引起了我的注意，
我在此想要詢問這個職缺。

**As your help-wanted ad caught my attention,
I am here to inquire about the position.**

重點文法 01

・原因與讓步句型：

As/Because/Though/ Even though	+	主詞 + 動詞, S V	原形＋動詞 S V

▶ 關鍵技巧與例句搶先看 01

了解英文中原因與讓步句型的運用

❶ 由於您的徵人啟事引起了我的注意，我在此想要詢問這個職缺。

As your help-wanted ad caught my attention, I am here to **inquire** about the position.

❷ 儘管我缺乏經驗，但是我有強烈的動機和抱負來發揮我最大的潛力。

Even though I am inexperienced, I am very **motivated** and ambitious to make the most of my **potentiality**.

▶ 相關文法說明

❶ 「As your help-wanted ad caught my attention, I am here to inquire about the position.」此句用到表示原因的句型：

★ **說明**：附屬連接詞 as, because, since, …等可引導表示原因的副詞子句。**句型**：As/Because＋主詞 (S)＋動詞 (V)，主詞 (S)＋動詞 (V)

★ **其他例句**：介系詞片語 owing to, due to, because of,…等後面則要接名詞，也可以有相同的語意及作用。

I'm keen to develop further in your company	owing to	the **well-rounded** welfare and the challenging work you offer.
S + be V + adj + to V	prep phr	n and n

由於貴公司所提供完善的福利制度和具挑戰性的工作，我很熱切地希望能在貴公司有進一步的發展。

❷ 「Even though I am inexperienced, I am very motivated and ambitious to make the most of my potentiality.」此句用到表示讓步的句型：

★ **說明**：though, even though, even if, …等可引導表示讓步的副詞子句。**句型**：(Even) Though＋主詞 (S)＋動詞 (V)，主詞 (S)＋動詞 (V)

★ **其他例句**：附屬連接詞引導的副詞子句可置於後。

Through Terry's **recommendation**,	I hope to inquire about the **vacancy**,	though I'm in fine **relationship** with my present employer.
prep + n	S+ V+ to VR+ prep+ n	though + S + be V + prep + n

經由泰瑞的推薦，雖然我與目前的老闆關係良好，我想要詢問有關於這個職缺的狀況。

▶ 相關的句型

● ～的原因是～：

The reason why +	主詞 + 動詞 + be 動詞 that + 主詞＋動詞
	S V be V that S V

The reason why I would like to **interview** for any position overseas is that I want to take on any **challenge** to stay ahead.

我想要有海外職缺面試機會的理由是我想接受任何挑戰來追求進步。

● 無論是～或是～，……：

Whether＋主詞＋be 動詞＋名詞＋	介系詞＋名詞 or 介系詞＋名詞,	主詞＋動詞
Whether S be V n	prep n or prep n,	S V

Whether it's a vacancy **in** a **retail** outlet **or** **in** a wholesale market, I will take it.

無論是零售商店或是批發市場的職缺，我都願意接受。

▶ 好用單字整理

	單字	詞性	中譯
1.	inquire	*v.*	訊問；查問
2.	motivated	*adj.*	有動機的；有積極性的
3.	potentiality	*n.*	潛力；可能性
4.	well-rounded	*adj.*	周全的；面面俱到的
5.	recommendation	*n.*	推薦；介紹
6.	vacancy	*n.*	空缺；空虛
7.	relationship	*n.*	關係；關聯
8.	interview	*v.*	面談；面試
9.	challenge	*n.*	挑戰；艱鉅任務
10.	retail	*n.*	零售（業）

4-2
Letters 英文信件 2：詢問信用語

我寄這封電子郵件的目的是想要詢問貨
物的運輸以及你們所提供的售後服務。
**I'm sending this e-mail so as to inquire about the goods
shipment and the after-sales service you provide.**

重點文法 02

目的與結果句型：

・表目的：

主詞 + 動詞 +	in order to/so as to +	原形動詞
S　　　V		VR

・表結果：

主詞 + 動詞 +	so ... that +	主詞 + 動詞
S　　　V		S　　　V

▶ 關鍵技巧與例句搶先看 02

了解英文中目的與結果句型的運用

❶ 我寄這封電子郵件的目的是想要詢問貨物的運輸以及你們所
提供的售後服務。

I'm sending this e-mail so as to inquire about the goods
shipment and the **after-sales** service you provide.

❷ 你們最新研發的產品是如此地知名以致於我們想要了解購買
貴商品的可能性。

Chapter 4 信件

4-2 ｜英文信件 2－詢問信用語 － 搭配文法：目的與結果句型

Part

1

句型篇

Part

2

圖解應用篇

Your newly developed products are so well-known that we would like to know about the possibility of making a **purchase**.

▶ 相關文法說明

❶ 「I'm sending this e-mail so as to inquire about the goods shipment and the after-sales service you provide.」此句用到表示目的的句型：

★ **說明**：不定詞片語 in order to, so as to, …等可用以表示目的。**句型**：主詞 (S)＋動詞 (V)＋in order to/so as to＋原形動詞 (VR)

★ **其他例句**：附屬連接詞片語 so that 接子句也可用以表示目的。

Please **advise** us of the exact date of **delivery**	so that	we	can place orders.
Please + VR + O + of + n	so that	S	aux + V + O

請告知確切的運送日期，如此我們便可以下訂單。

❷ 「Your newly developed products are so well-known that we would like to know about the possibility of making a purchase.」是表結果的句型：

★ **說明**：附屬連接詞片語 so ... that 接子句用以表示結果。**句型**：主詞 (S)＋動詞 (V)＋so + adj/adv + that＋主詞 (S)＋動詞 (V)

★ 其他例句：連接詞式的副詞 thus, hence, consequently, therefore... 等表示結果的語意，前面加分號後，可用以連接子句。

I'm interested in your hi-tech products;	consequently,	I hope to get the related **information** you may offer.
S + beV + adj + prep + n	adv	S + V + to + VR + O

我對於您的高科技產品深感興趣；因此，我希望能得到貴公司可以提供的相關資訊。

▶ 相關的句型

● 為了要……：

For the purpose of/With a view to + n/v.ing...,	主詞＋動詞
	S V

For the **purpose** of **establishing** a business relationship soon, could we get your reply before July 1?

為了儘快建立商業關係，我們可以在七月一日前得到您的答覆嗎？

● ～ 足夠 ～ 可以讓某人 ～：

主詞＋動詞＋adj/adv	enough	for 某人	to	原形動詞
S V adj/adv	enough	for somebody to		VR

Please provide us with the latest **catalog** and your best prices early enough for us to refer to.

請儘早提供我們最新的目錄以及最好的價格以供參考。

▶ 好用單字整理

	單字	詞性	中譯
1.	shipment	*n.*	裝運；運送
2.	after-sales	*adj.*	（出）售後的
3.	purchase	*n.*	購買；採購
4.	advise	*v.*	通知；告知
5.	delivery	*n.*	遞送；交貨
6.	consequently	*adv.*	結果；因此
7.	information	*n.*	消息；資訊
8.	purpose	*n.*	目的；用途
9.	establish	*v.*	建立；創辦
10.	catalog	*n.*	目錄（冊）

4-3
Letters 英文信件 3：請求信用語

經過仔細的考慮後，我們樂於指定貴公司擔任我們區域性的業務代理公司。

After careful consideration, we are delighted to appoint your company as our regional sales agency.

重點文法 03

時間與條件句型：

・表時間句型：

Before/After/Since +	名詞,	主詞 +	動詞
	n,	S	V

・表條件句型：

If +	主詞 +	動詞,	主詞 +	助動詞 +	動詞
If	S	V,	S	aux	V

▶ 關鍵技巧與例句搶先看 03

了解英文中時間與條件句型的運用

❶ 經過仔細的考慮後，我們樂於指定貴公司擔任我們區域性的業務代理公司。

After careful **consideration**, we are delighted to appoint your company as our **regional** sales agency.

❷ 假使貴公司給我們機會販售您的商品，對我們雙方來說，將會有滿意的結果。

If you agree to give us an **opportunity** to sell your products, the results will be **satisfactory** to both of us.

▶ 相關文法說明

❶ 「After careful consideration, we are delighted to appoint your company as our regional sales agency.」此句用到表示時間的句型：

★ **說明**：介詞 before, after, since, …等後接名詞再接主要子句，說明時間。**句型**：Before/After/Since＋名詞 (n)，主詞 (S)＋動詞 (V)

★ **其他例句**：when、while、as soon as、……等引導表時間的附屬子句。

As soon as we	**notified** our clients of the new prices,	they complained about the high charge and **demanded** a reduction.
conj + S	V + O + of + O	S + V + prep + n

我們一通知客戶新價格，他們便對於高收費提出抱怨並要求減價。

❷ 「If you agree to give us an opportunity to sell your products, the results will be satisfactory to both of us.」此句用到表示條件的句型：

★ **說明**：連接詞 if, unless, providing (that), …等可引導表條件

的附屬子句。**句型**：If＋主詞 (S)＋動詞 (V)，主詞 (S)＋助動詞 (aux)＋動詞 (V)。

★ **其他例句**：wish 接不定詞片語或假設語氣子句也可以表示條件。

We wish	to find a company willing to **represent** us in your area	as long as you can recommend us some **reliable** sources.
S + wish	to + VR + O + OC	as long as + S + aux + VR + O

只要您可以為我們推薦一些信譽良好的來源，我們希望能夠在貴地找到願意代表我們的公司。

▶ 相關的句型

● 直到～才～：

It ＋ be 動詞 ＋ not until ＋ 主詞 ＋ 動詞 **that**	主詞＋動詞
It　be V　not until　S　V　that	**S**　**V**

It is not until you enclose with the necessary detailed prices and payment terms that we'll decide on **granting** your application.

直到您附上必要的價格細目以及付款條件，我們才會決定是否批准您的申請。

● 某人早就應該〜：

$$\text{It is high/about time that } + \frac{\text{假設語氣}}{\text{S + were/v-ed/should + VR}}$$

I regret to say that it's high time you (should) improve your after-sales service, or we might **decline** your request again.

我很遺憾地說，貴公司早就應該改善你們的售後服務，否則我們很可能將再度婉拒您的請求。

▶ 好用單字整理

	單字	詞性	中譯
1.	consideration	*n.*	考慮；深思
2.	regional	*adj.*	區域的；地區的
3.	opportunity	*n.*	機會；良機
4.	satisfactory	*adj.*	不滿意的；不夠理想的
5.	notify	*v.*	通知；告知
6.	demand	*v.*	要求；請求
7.	represent	*v.*	代表；代理
8.	reliable	*adj.*	可信賴的；可靠的
9.	grant	*v.*	同意；准許
10.	decline	*v.*	婉拒；謝絕

4-4
Letters 英文信件 4：抱怨信用語

我一點都沒想到向貴公司購買的數
位電話的顯示面竟然有問題。

Little did I expect to find the LED display of the digital
phone purchased from your company went wrong.

重點文法 04

強調與焦點句型：

· 強調句型：

副詞	+	助動詞	+	主詞	+	原形動詞
adv		aux		S		VR

· 焦點句型：

主詞	+	never	+	動詞	+	受詞	+	without	+	名詞
S		never		V		O		without		N

▶ 關鍵技巧與例句搶先看 04

了解英文中強調與焦點句型的運用

❶ 我一點都沒想到向貴公司購買的數位電話的顯示面竟然有問
題。

Little did I expect to find the LED **display** of the digital phone
purchased from your company went wrong.

❷ 恐怕您不改善延遲付款的狀況，我們將無法進行進一步的商
品運送。

I am afraid that we'll never make any **further** goods shipment without your **improvement** of the slow payment.

▶ 相關文法說明

❶ 「Little did I expect to find the LED display of the digital phone purchased from your company went wrong.」此句用到表示強調的句型：

★ **說明**：否定副詞 no, little, seldom, hardly, …等可置於句首倒裝，加強語氣。**句型**：副詞 (adv)＋助動詞 (aux)＋主詞 (S)＋原形動詞 (VR)

★ **其他例句**：no sooner...than... 為連接詞片語可倒裝以加強語氣。

No sooner	had I found	a metal chip in my steak	than I asked for the waiter's immediate make-up action, only to find it **unsatisfactory**.
No sooner	aux + S + V	O	than + S + V + prep + O

我一發現我的牛排裡有一片金屬碎片，就請服務生做立即的補救措施，但得到的仍是不滿意的結果。

❷ 「I am afraid that we'll never make any further goods shipment without your improvement of the slow payment.」此句用到表示焦點的句型：

★ 說明：never... without ...（沒有……不……）雙重否定，表示強調的訊息焦點。**句型**：主詞 (S)＋never＋動詞 (V)＋受詞 (O)＋without＋名詞 (N)

★ **其他例句**：what 子句可形成分裂句強調主詞或補語的訊息焦點。

What we originally expected from you	was	that the products shipped should meet our **quality standards**.
What + S + V	beV	that + S + aux + VR + O

我們原先對貴公司的期盼是運送的貨品應該要能符合我們對於品質標準的要求。

▶ 相關的句型

● 「假使～，～將～」：假設語氣中，省略 if 後可倒裝以加強語氣：

be 動詞＋主詞,	主詞＋	助動詞	＋原形動詞
Were　　S	S	would/could/should/might	VR

Were you not able to **resolve** this matter as quickly as possible, we probably would have to ask for **compensation** from you.

假使您無法儘速解決這個問題，我們很可能必須向貴公司求償。

● 「是～才是～」為分裂句句型：**It is/was ... that ...** 用以強調訊息焦點：

It is/was ＋ 加強的主詞／受詞／副詞 ＋ that ＋ 句子其餘的部份
It is/was   S/O/adv   that...

It is your promise of future **promptness** and a written agreement for late **penalty** fees that could motivate us to go on placing orders.

唯有您允諾日後快速出貨，並且附上延遲出貨的賠償協議，我們才有意願繼續下訂單。

▶ 好用單字整理

	單字	詞性	中譯
1.	digital	*adj.*	數字的；數位的
2.	further	*adj.*	更遠的；進一步的
3.	improvement	*n.*	改善；改進
4.	unsatisfactory	*adj.*	令人不滿的；不符合要求的
5.	quality	*n.*	品質；特質
6.	standard	*n.*	標準；水準
7.	resolve	*v.*	解決；解答
8.	compensation	*n.*	補償；賠償
9.	promptness	*n.*	迅速；快速
10.	penalty	*n.*	處罰；罰款

4-5
Letters 英文信件 5：回覆信用語
由於經濟蕭條，恐怕今年公司的利潤會比去年來的低。

Due to the economic recession, I'm afraid that the company profit of this year will be lower than that of last year.

重點文法 05

比較與對比句型：

・比較句型：

主詞 + 動詞 + 形容詞～er/more + 形容詞 than + 主詞
S　　　V　　　　adj.～er/more adj. than　　　S

・對比句型：

As opposed to +	名詞, + 主詞 + 動詞 + 受詞
	N,　　S　　V　　O

▶ 關鍵技巧與例句搶先看 05

了解英文中比較與對比句型的運用

❶ 由於經濟蕭條，恐怕今年公司的利潤會比去年來的低。

Due to the economic **recession**, I'm afraid that the company **profit** of this year will be lower than that of last year.

❷ 相對於其他公司較低的價格，我提議我們應該把價格降低兩成。

As opposed to other company's lower prices, I **propose** that we should reduce the prices by 20%.

▶ 相關文法說明

❶ 「Due to the economic recession, I'm afraid that the company profit of this year will be lower than that of last year.」此句用到比較的句型：

★ **說明**：使用比較級形容詞比較時，單音節字字尾加 er，多音節字時是 more＋形容詞原級，再用連接詞 than 連結前後子句。**句型**：主詞 (S)＋動詞 (V)＋形容詞～er/more＋形容詞＋than…

★ **其他例句**：good 形容詞比較時，屬於不規則變化，最高級是 best。

This is our company's most **functional** printer on the market,	so the best offer I can make	is 5% **discount**.
S + be V + SC	so + the best + n	be V + SC

這是我們公司在市場上功用最多的印表機，所以我能夠提供最好的折扣是九五折。

❷ 「As opposed to other company's lower prices, I propose that we should reduce the prices by 20%.」此句用到對比的句型：

★ **說明**：表示相反、對照的用字及片語有 unlike、whereas、

coversely、far from、contrast with、rather than、instead of、on the contrary……等。句型：As opposed to＋名詞 (N)，主詞 (S)＋動詞 (V)＋受詞 (O)

★ 其他例句：rather than/instead of 是表示相反、對照的片語。

Rather than	giving a **refund** to the customer complaining about the phone,	we decided to send her a **replacement**.
Rather than	v.ing + O	S + V + to + VR + O

我們決定寄送替代的新電話給那位提出抱怨的客戶，而非退款給她。

▶ 相關的句型

• 「～是～的～倍」表示「倍數比較」的句型：可使用的倍數詞有 **half**、**twice**、**three times**、**four times** 等。

……倍數詞 as many		＋名詞＋as …
可使用的倍數詞有 half、twice、three times、four times 等。		n as...

As we cut down on our prices this year, our company has so far received three times as many orders as last year.

因為今年我們的產品降價，我們公司到目前為止收到的訂單是去年的三倍。

● 「雖然～，但是相反地，～」表示「相反、對照」的句型：

連接詞＋主詞＋動詞＋受詞,＋				on the contrary / by contrast,	主詞＋動詞＋受詞
Though	S	V	O		S＋V＋O ……

Though you show great **confidence** in your products, by contrast, the **similar** products made by your **competitor** are better but cheaper.

雖然您對您的產品有信心，但相反地，您的對手公司所製造類似的產品品質更好，但是價格更便宜。

▶ 好用單字整理

	單字	詞性	中譯
1.	recession	*n.*	（經濟的）衰退；不景氣
2.	profit	*n.*	利潤；收益
3.	propose	*v.*	提議；建議
4.	functional	*adj.*	機能的；作用的
5.	discount	*n.*	折扣；打折
6.	refund	*n.*	退款；償還金額
7.	replacement	*n.*	更換；代替（物）
8.	confidence	*n.*	自信；信心
9.	similar	*adj.*	類似的；相似的
10.	competitor	*n.*	競爭者；對手

Part 1 句型篇

Part 2 圖解應用篇

4-6
Letters 英文信件 6：感謝信用語

我們感謝過去您提供的服務，藉由附上的新合約，我想通知您我們未來將持續合作。

We appreciate the service you provided, and with the enclosed new contract, I'd inform you of our future cooperation.

重點文法 06

• 特殊動詞句型：

主詞	+	及物動詞	+	某人	+	介系詞	+	某物
S		Vt		sb		of		sth

注意：容易誤用動詞的特性和中文應分辨清楚，做正確的選擇與使用。如 rise（上升）及 arise（發生）是不及物動詞，後面不接受詞。rouse（叫醒）及 arouse（激起）是及物動詞，後面要接受詞等。

▶ 關鍵技巧與例句搶先看 06

了解英文中特殊動詞句型的運用

❶ 我們感謝過去您提供的服務，藉由附上的新合約，我想通知您我們未來將持續合作。

We appreciate the service you provided, and with the enclosed new **contract**, I'd inform you of our future **cooperation**.

❷ 您持續的支持引起我們與您進一步合作的興趣，我們也感謝您對我們展現的信心。

Your constant support arouses our interest in further cooperation with you, and we thank you for your confidence in us.

▶ 相關文法說明

❶「We appreciate the service you provided, and with the enclosed new contract, I'd inform you of our future cooperation.」動詞 inform 句型：

★ **說明**：特殊動詞，應注意使用規則、固定意義，及用法，力求正確。如：inform、notify、remind、convince、persuade 等須搭配介詞 of 使用。**句型**：主詞 (S)＋及物動詞 (Vt)＋某人 (sb)＋介系詞 (of)＋某物 (sth)

★ **其他例句**：keep/stop/prevent + sb + from + sth（防止～做～）

To keep our relationship from becoming **distant**,	please accept the gifts	and **attend** our Annual Appreciation **Banquet**.
To keep + n + from + v.ing	please +VR + O	and + VR + O

期盼我們的關係可以更加緊密，請收下贈禮，並出席我們舉辦的年度感恩宴會。

❷「Your constant support arouses our interest in further cooperation with you, and we thank you for your confidence in us.」動詞 arouse 的句型：

★ **說明**：arise 是不及物動詞，不接受詞。arouse 是及物動詞，要接受詞。動詞 arouse 的句型：主詞 (S)＋及物動詞 (arouse)＋受詞 (O)

★ 其他例句：reply/response + to + O（回覆～），接 to，再接受詞。

Many thanks for your **prompt** reply to	our new **proposal**, and through cooperation,	we look forward to future **promising prospects**.
S + prep + reply + to	O, and prep + O,	S + V + prep + O

非常感謝您快速地回覆我們的新提案，經由合作，我們可預期未來看好的前景。

▶ 相關的句型

- 「把～視為～」屬特殊動詞句型：regard/view/see/think of/look upon/refer to～as～

We **regard** it **as** an honor that you chose us **as** your supplier for the past year, and we wish to express our thanks.

我們把過去一年您選擇我們擔任您的供應商視為一項榮耀，我們想表達我們的謝意。

- 特殊動詞 **spend**、**take**、**cost** 的用法：某人花時間或花錢用 spend，接動名詞 (v.ing)。it 當主詞時，花時間用 take，花錢用 cost，接不定詞 (to V)。（人＋spend＋時間＋(in) V-ing＝It take ＋人＋時間＋to V；人＋spend＋金錢＋on 物品＝It cost＋人＋金錢＋to V）

We feel much **obliged** to you for the time your company spent and the efforts made in building up markets for our new products.

我們非常感謝您在開拓我們新產品的市場上付出的時間和努力。

▶ 好用單字整理

	單字	詞性	中譯
1.	contract	*n.*	契約；合約
2.	cooperation	*n.*	合作；協力
3.	distant	*adj.*	遙遠的；疏離的
4.	attend	*v.*	出席；參加
5.	banquet	*n.*	宴會；盛宴
6.	proposal	*n.*	提議；提案
7.	promising	*adj.*	有前途的；大有可為的
8.	prospect	*n.*	願景；前途
9.	regard	*v.*	看作；考慮
10.	obliged	*adj.*	感激的

4-7

英文信件用語句型小練習

▶ 英文信件用語句型小回顧

　　在書寫英文信時，句型方面，除了五大基本句型外，經常運用到由附屬連接詞所引導以表示各種作用的副詞子句，譬如表明原因與讓步、時間與條件、目的與結果、強調與焦點、比較與對比等，另外特殊動詞句型亦是應該仔細區分辨別的一個類型。只要熟悉使用英文書信固定的字彙、片語，及文法，加上活用固定搭配的常用語及句型，撰寫信件將輕鬆容易多了。

▶ 文法句型補一補

( ) 1. _____ did Mark imagine entering his ideal college.

    (A) Not   (B) Little   (C) Always   (D) Till

( ) 2. It was _____ this morning that David was informed of the request.

    (A) no longer   (B) not yet   (C) no more   (D) not until

( ) 3. _____ your hotel provided bad service, I am calling to complain.

    (A) Before   (B) Though   (C) Because   (D) Thus

( ) 4. Mr. Hanks _____ it as an honor to make a speech in the banquet.

    (A) heard   (B) watched   (C) regarded   (D) looked

( ) 5. Our company is presenting our goods in the Trade Fair now _____ promote its sales.

    (A) due to   (B) in order to

    (C) such that   (D) so that

( ) 6. Sales have dropped recently, which resulted in the much _____ payment than before.

    (A) slower   (B) slow   (C) slowest   (D) slowly

▶ 答案與解析

1. (B) Little

題目中譯 馬克幾乎不敢想像他能夠進入他理想的大學。

答案解析 否定副詞 little 置於句首倒裝，加強語氣。Little 後接助動詞 did 搭配原形動詞 imagine，故應選 (B) Little。

2. (D) not until

題目中譯 直到今天早上，大衛才被告知這項請求。

答案解析 It＋be 動詞＋not until＋名詞＋that＋主詞＋動詞……（直到～才～）是 not until 的固定句型。故應選 (D) not until。

3. (C) Because

題目中譯 由於貴旅館提供劣質的服務，我打這通電話來抱怨。

答案解析 附屬連接詞 because 引導表示原因的副詞子句。故應選 (C) Because。

4. (C) regarded

題目中譯 漢克斯先生把在宴會中演講視為一項榮譽。

答案解析 特殊動詞 regard～as～（把～視為～）是固定句型。故應選 (C) regarded。

5. (B) in order to

題目中譯 我們公司現在正在貿易展覽會場上展示我們的商品來促銷。

答案解析 不定詞片語 in order to 用以表示目的。故應選 (B) in order to。

6. (A) slower

題目中譯 最近銷售量大減，這導致比往常更延遲的付款。

答案解析 使用比較級形容詞比較時，單音節字字尾加 er，再用連接詞 than 連結前後子句。故應選 (A) slower。

▶ 寫作老師巧巧說

在書寫英文信件時，要能遵守準確、簡潔，及清晰的原則，應避免累贅文字，重要的是英文用字、片語、文法，及句型的使用更要力求正確得宜，便可達到有效的溝通及訊息的傳達，寫出成功的英文書信。一封英文信應包含開頭、本文，以及結尾三大部份，正確的文法觀念及實用達意的句型架構可提升信件的可讀性，所以仔細瞭解熟悉句型語法，並將文法句型整體活用，是寫好英文書信的關鍵。

Part 2
圖解應用篇

本部份 36 篇文章，運用 Part 1 句型篇學習到的句型，
提供撰寫英文報告、作文、自傳和信件的寫作技巧及範文。
依各個主題利用圖解的方式呈現寫作的架構，有助於分了解
該類型文章的寫法。寫作原則及技巧分析解說文章類型，並
有各段文章的摘要說明及寫作重點，可印證寫作方式及技
巧。正確運用靈活的文法句型、精準確實的用字遣詞，加上
卓越的寫作技巧，佳作便呼之欲出了。

1-1
應徵「導遊」英文自傳結合「大自然生活描述」句型應用

搭配文法：五大基本句型

▶ 圖解寫作架構

應徵職業（Applying Job）

A Tour Guide 導遊

家庭背景與影響（Family Background and Influences）

Born into a family of four members, I often get close to nature with my family. 家中有四名成員，我常與家人接近大自然。

教育與工作經驗（Education and Working Experiences）

Before finishing all the major courses, I used to coach summer camps as part-time jobs. 我在修完所有主修課程前，過去常常兼差指導夏令營。

興趣與技能（Interests and Skills）

I love traveling and making friends, and I'm a licensed tour guide mastering several foreign languages. 我熱愛旅遊及交友，並且是精通數國外語、領有執照的導遊。

態度與期許（Attitudes and Expectations）

Being optimistic and responsible, I hope to fulfill my dreams of traveling and helping tourists enjoy their trips. 樂觀負責的我希望能實現旅遊及幫助觀光客享受旅程的夢想。

▶ 圖解重點說分明

關於應徵「導遊」英文自傳的書寫

重點：應徵職業的自傳可由描述應徵者的「家庭背景與影響」，「教育與工作經驗」，「興趣與技能」，以及「態度與期許」四方面對自己做完整且令人印象深刻的介紹，強調自己是理想稱職的人選。

❶ 「**Born into a family of four members, I often get close to nature with my family.**」說明應徵者的家庭背景對他日後喜愛旅遊產生重大影響。

❷ 「**Before finishing all the major courses, I used to coach summer camps as part-time jobs.**」此部份強調應徵者大學教育與打工經驗兼具。

❸ 「**I love traveling and making friends, and I'm a licensed tour guide mastering several foreign languages.**」興趣與技能兩者的結合有益工作的進行。

❹ 「**Being optimistic and responsible, I hope to fulfill my dreams of traveling and helping tourists enjoy their trips.**」態度與期許的強調作為結論，企盼能由此成功求職。

英文自傳 便利貼光碟 1-1 Tips：實線和虛線是可以替換的地方，虛線同時也是單元重要句型，套色處結合 Part 1 句型文法的應用，整合式學習拓展寫作能力！

An Autobiography

I am Henry Li, aged twenty-five. Born into a family of four members, I often get close to nature with my family. As nature-lovers, my parents often took my brother and me to go on short trips in the countryside when we were little. So, I have become fond of traveling around whenever possible.

I consider myself lucky to major in Tourism in college. Before finishing all the major courses, I used to coach summer camps as part-time jobs. During those hot summer days, I enjoyed swimming in the lake, climbing mountains, and going on hikes with young children.

I am humorous, passionate, and communicative. I love traveling and making friends, and I'm a licensed tour guide mastering several foreign languages. I am good at English, Japanese, and Korean. After diligent studying, I have got the certificate of tour guide and am now an official licensed tour guide. Furthermore, I always work energetically.

I hold positive attitudes toward life. Being optimistic and responsible, I hope to fulfill my dreams of traveling and helping tourists enjoy their trips. I am completing my military service this July and I want to become a top-notch tour guide. I will see the wonderful world myself and bring happiness and knowledge to tourists while showing them the natural scenery and historic relics all over the world.

自傳

我是李亨利，二十五歲。家中有四名成員，我常與家人接近大自然。身為大自然的愛好者，我的父母在我們年幼時，時常帶著我和我的哥哥到鄉間去做短程旅遊。於是，我變得喜歡一有機會就到處旅遊。

我很幸運在大學時主修觀光系。我在修完所有主修課程前，過去常常兼差指導夏令營。在炎炎夏日時，我非常喜歡和小孩子們在湖裡游泳，爬山，以及健行。

我生性幽默、熱情，並且善於與人溝通。我熱愛旅遊及交友，並且是精通數國外語、領有執照的導遊。我精通英文，日文，和韓文。經過勤勉苦讀後，我得到了導遊證照，現在是一名正式領有執照的導遊。再者，我總是活力十足地工作。

我對人生抱持著正面積極的態度。樂觀負責的我希望能實現旅遊及幫助觀光客享受旅程的夢想。今年七月，我將服完兵役，我想成為一名一流的導遊。我將親自一睹美妙的世界，並且在帶領觀光客環遊世界觀賞自然美景和歷史古蹟時，帶給他們快樂及知識。

1-2
應徵「景觀設計師」英文自傳
結合「鄉間生活描述」句型應用
搭配文法：動詞時態

▶ **圖解寫作架構**

應徵職業（Applying Job）

A Landscape Architect 景觀設計師

家庭背景與影響（Family Background and Influences）

Born in a small town in Taiwan, I have loved horticulture owing to my early childhood working experiences. 出生於台灣的一個小城鎮，我因早期童年的工作經驗，愛上了園藝。

教育與工作經驗（Education and Working Experiences）

While studying in college as a Landscape Architecture major, I worked part-time as a horticulture assistant. 我在大學時主修景觀設計，同時打工兼差做園藝助理。

興趣與技能（Interests and Skills）

Besides my interests for horticultural work, I am quite a qualified landscape architect. 除了我在園藝工作上的興趣之外，我是一個相當稱職的景觀設計師。

態度與期許（Attitudes and Expectations）

Always looking on the bright side of life, I expect to broaden my horizons. 我生性樂觀，期盼能更上一層樓。

▶ 圖解重點說分明

關於應徵「景觀設計師」英文自傳的書寫

重點：應徵者除了學歷、經驗，及技能外，特佳的人格特質，如熱愛生命，執著於愛護地球的理念，並持續努力保持永續生態環境的遠見及作法，顯示是位可長期栽培，並將固守崗位的優秀人員。

❶「**Born in a small town in Taiwan, I have loved horticulture owing to my early childhood working experiences.**」說明應徵者童年的農場工作經驗對他日後喜愛園藝及景觀設計有重大影響。

❷「**While studying in college as a Landscape Architecture major, I worked part-time as a horticulture assistant.**」園藝助理打工的工作伴隨景觀設計的主修學用合一。

❸「**Besides my interests for horticultural work, I am quite a qualified landscape architect.**」兼具對於園藝的興趣與合格景觀設計師實際操作的技能令人印象深刻。

❹「**Always looking on the bright side of life, I expect to broaden my horizons.**」樂觀進取的學習態度與企盼更上一層樓的企圖心有助於塑造好的形象。

英文自傳 便利貼光碟 1-2 Tips：實線和虛線是可以替換的地方，虛線同時也是單元重要句型，套色處結合 Part 1 句型文法的應用，整合式學習拓展寫作能力！

An Autobiography

I am Mark Tang, and I am twenty-six. I live with my wife, who I fell in love with and married in college, and my little daughter. Born in a small town in Taiwan, I have loved horticulture owing to my early childhood working experiences. I started working on my family's garden farm when little and have loved doing horticultural jobs since then.

While studying in college as a Landscape Architecture major, I worked part-time as a horticulture assistant. I took summer jobs of working in Peterson Company as a horticulture assistant. Also, I did assistant work designing and creating sustainable and pleasing environments around gardens, parks, buildings, and so on.

I love to take care of flower gardens, fruit plantations, and appreciate life on land. Besides my interests for horticultural work, I am quite a qualified landscape architect. With formal college qualifications, I have good design skills in using Computer-Aided Design (CAD). In addition, I have excellent communication and negotiating skills.

I am imaginative, hard-working and highly responsible. After one month, I am going to complete my military service. Always looking on the bright side of life, I expect to broaden my horizons. I will try my best to seek greater chances to enter a bigger company and further my ambition.

自傳

我是唐馬克，二十六歲。我和我大學時期相戀結婚的妻子以及我的小女兒住在一起。出生於台灣的一個小城鎮，我因早期童年的工作經驗，愛上了園藝。我小時候便開始在家族的花園農場上工作，並且從那時起喜歡做園藝的工作。

我在大學時主修景觀設計，同時打工兼差做園藝助理。在暑假時，我曾在彼得森公司擔任園藝助理。此外，我也做設計助理的工作，在花園、公園、建築物等等周遭創造永續且宜人的環境。

我喜歡照料花園、果園，並且欣賞土地上的生命。除了我在園藝工作上的興趣之外，我是一個相當稱職的景觀設計師。我有正式的大學學歷；我擅長使用電腦繪圖軟體。再者，我有絕佳的溝通及協商的技能。

我富有想像力、勤奮努力，並且具有高度的責任感。一個月後，我即將退伍。我生性樂觀，期盼能更上一層樓。我將盡最大的力量尋找更佳的機會進入更大的公司，以伸展我的抱負。

1-3
應徵「攝影師」英文自傳結合「街景描寫」句型應用

搭配文法：主動與被動語態

▶ 圖解寫作架構

應徵職業（Applying Job）

A Photographer 攝影師

家庭背景與影響（Family Background and Influences）

With four members in our family, my younger sister and I were raised in a liberal style. 家中有四名成員，我妹妹和我成長於自由開放的家庭環境中。

教育與工作經驗（Education and Working Experiences）

From joining school Club of Photography and working part-time in Fantasy Photo Studio, I learned a lot about photography. 加入學校的攝影社以及在夢幻攝影公司打工時，我學到許多攝影技巧。

興趣與技能（Interests and Skills）

Photography offers me great pleasure, and I am equipped with great professional skills. 攝影帶給我極大的樂趣，並且我具備絕佳的專業技術。

態度與期許（Attitudes and Expectations）

With great enthusiasm, I wish to be a freelance photographer in the future. 帶著極大的熱忱，我希望未來能成為一名自由攝影師。

圖解重點說分明

關於應徵「攝影師」英文自傳的書寫

重點：社會新鮮人無正式的專職經驗，唸大學時曾有與應徵職業相關的社團及打工經驗，對應徵者來說是非常重要且關鍵的。在自傳求職的書寫中務必提及並且強調，將會有極佳的加分作用。

❶「**With four members in our family, my younger sister and I were raised in a liberal style.**」父母親關愛且開放的教養方式使得應徵者具有富創意、樂觀的個性。

❷「**From joining school Club of Photography and working part-time in Fantasy Photo Studio, I learned a lot about photography.**」應徵者經由社團活動與打工經驗在攝影技術上多所涉獵學習。

❸「**Photography offers me great pleasure, and I am equipped with great professional skills.**」對於攝影的喜愛與專門技能兩者的結合說明應徵者足以勝任攝影師的工作。

❹「**With great enthusiasm, I wish to be a freelance photographer in the future.**」應徵者的熱忱與勇於接受新攝影工作挑戰的態度強調自己能勝任任何賦予他的工作。

Part 1 句型篇

Part 2 圖解應用篇

133

英文自傳 便利貼光碟 1-3 Tips：實線和虛線是可以替換的地方，虛線同時也是單元重要句型，套色處結合 Part 1 句型文法的應用，整合式學習拓展寫作能力！

An Autobiography

I am Jason Lin, aged twenty-four. With four members in our family, my younger sister and I were raised in a liberal style. My parents are caring and open-minded, always ready to offer us help and encouragement. The close family relationship inspired me to become creative and responsible.

I was a physics major in college, and it was taken for granted that I would be interested in things related to physics. However, I took great interest in taking photos. From joining school Club of Photography and working part-time in Fantasy Photo Studio, I learned a lot about photography. In the club, I recorded the beauty of both the rural and the urban scenes. In senior year's studio job, I strengthened my shooting ability.

Photography offers me great pleasure, and I am equipped with great professional skills. I have a good command of computer software, such as AutoCAD, Illustrator, Photoshop, etc. I am good at retouching pictures, editing, and filming videos for special occasions like weddings. Also, I know how to maintain equipment and interact smoothly with my clients.

I am <u>optimistic, creative, and hard-working</u> in fulfilling missions and goals in life. <u>With great enthusiasm, I wish to be a freelance photographer in the future.</u> I would like to explore a new working world and will be eager to take up new photography projects and face challenges.

自傳

我是林傑生，二十四歲。家中有四名成員，我妹妹和我成長於自由開放的家庭環境中。我的雙親對子女十分關愛開放，並隨時給予我們協助和鼓勵。這種密切的家庭關係激勵我成為具創意且富責任感的人。

我大學時主修物理，理所當然地，我應該對與物理相關的事物有興趣。然而，我對於攝影有極大的興趣。加入學校的攝影社以及在夢幻攝影公司打工時，我學到許多攝影技巧。在社團中，我紀錄了鄉間與都會的美景。在大四時的攝影工作中，我增進了我的攝影能力。

攝影帶給我極大的樂趣，並且我具備絕佳的專業技術。我擅長使用電腦軟體，像 AutoCAD、Illustrator、以及 Photoshop 等等。我精通於修片、編輯，以及替特殊場合，像婚禮，拍攝錄影帶。此外，我知道如何維修機器，及如何順暢地和我的客戶互動。

我在完成任務以及實現人生目標上樂觀、具創意、而且肯苦幹。帶著極大的熱忱，我希望未來能成為一名自由攝影師。我想要拓展新的工作領域，我將熱切地接受新的攝影計劃並且面對挑戰。

1-4
應徵「電視廣告撰稿員」英文自傳
結合「電視優缺點描述」句型應用

搭配文法：助動詞句型

▶ **圖解寫作架構**

應徵職業（Applying Job）

A TV Commercial Copywriter 電視廣告撰稿員

家庭背景與影響（Family Background and Influences）

Born and raised in a very traditional family, I am quite an introvert. 生長於一個非常傳統的家庭中，我的個性十分內向。

教育與工作經驗（Education and Working Experiences）

I've learned much from both college courses and the assistant experiences. 我從大學課程和做助理的經驗中學到很多。

興趣與技能（Interests and Skills）

Due to the great passion for media, I have tried hard to increase basic TV commercial writing skills. 基於對大眾媒體的熱愛，我努力嘗試增強基本的電視廣告撰寫技巧。

態度與期許（Attitudes and Expectations）

I am strongly motivated to learn and am aimed to exert my media potentiality by developing my own copywriting realm. 我有強烈的學習動機並且有志於發展我自己的文章風格來發揮媒體潛能。

圖解重點說分明

關於應徵「電視廣告撰稿員」英文自傳的書寫

重點：應徵者文筆佳，視野廣，興趣廣泛，又肯努力學習，是可栽培的好人才。在自傳中闡述理念及向學的意願，再加上學歷佳，撰稿技能、潛力強，往往是求才工作主管願雇用的人員。

❶「**Born and raised in a very traditional family, I am quite an introvert.**」說明應徵者內向、喜好閱讀及寫作的個性和出生於傳統式家庭教育有關。

❷「**I've learned much from both college courses and the assistant experiences.**」大眾傳播之主修與電視台及電視廣告撰稿的助理工作使得應徵者熟悉理論和實質的工作環境。

❸「**Due to the great passion for media, I have tried hard to obtain basic TV commercial writing skills.**」廣泛汲取大眾媒體知識及撰稿、校稿技巧的技能訓練足證應徵者能力甚佳。

❹「**I am strongly motivated to learn and am aimed to exert my media potentiality by developing my own copywriting realm.**」剛從大學畢業，應徵者有強烈的學習動機及遠大的抱負。更重要的是有自信可以自創風格。

Part 1 句型篇

Part 2 圖解應用篇

英文自傳 便利貼光碟 1-4 Tips：實線和虛線是可以替換的地方，虛線同時也是單元重要句型，套色處結合 Part 1 句型文法的應用，整合式學習拓展寫作能力！

An Autobiography

My name is Sharon Chang. I am twenty-three years old. Born and raised in a very traditional family, I am quite an introvert. I have loved to read novels and write articles since little. I am particularly fond of keeping a diary and reading all sorts of magazines for latest information.

I majored in Mass Communication in college. I've learned much from both college courses and the assistant experiences. I used to work in a TV station assisting some TV programs. Also, in my junior and senior years, I was employed as an assistant TV commercial copywriter.

I love to watch drama, sports, news, and documentaries on TV. In addition, I research and explore webs on the Internet. Due to the great passion for media, I have tried hard to increase basic TV commercial writing skills. I know how to write sales promotion ads and consumer ads, and I can proofread ads for copy and design errors.

As a college graduate for only a few months, I still have a

long way to go concerning media work and I had better do everything all out. However, I am strongly motivated to learn and am aimed to exert my media potentiality by developing my own writing style. If I am luckily employed by your commercial incorporation, I believe, through my catchy slogans, I can build up brands and promote sales for clients.

自傳

我是張雪倫，今年二十三歲。生長於一個非常傳統的家庭中，我的個性十分內向。自小我喜歡閱讀小說以及寫文章，尤其喜歡寫日記以及閱讀各種雜誌來得知最新訊息。

我大學時主修大眾傳播，我從大學課程和做助理的經驗中學到很多。我曾在電視台工作，負責協助某些電視節目。此外，大三大四時，我受雇擔任電視廣告助理撰稿員。

我喜歡觀看電視劇、運動節目、新聞，以及紀錄片。此外，我在網際網路上研究以及瀏覽網頁。基於對大眾媒體的熱愛，我努力嘗試增強基本的電視廣告撰寫技巧。我知道如何寫促銷產品的廣告和吸引消費者的廣告，同時我可以校出廣告中文案及設計的錯誤。

我大學剛畢業幾個月，就媒體工作來說，我還有很多需要努力的地方，而且，我最好全力以付。然而，我有強烈的學習動機並且有志於發展我自己的文章風格來發揮媒體潛能。假使我很幸運地被貴公司雇用，我相信，經由我吸引人的文案撰寫，我可以為客戶建立品牌，並且增進產品的銷售量。

1-5
應徵「電視影片翻譯員」英文自傳結合「電視節目」句型應用

搭配文法：不定詞句型

▶ 圖解寫作架構

應徵職業（Applying Job）

A Telefilm Translator 電視影片翻譯員

家庭背景與影響（Family Background and Influences）

Under their influences, it is natural for me to love reading and writing since little. 在他們的影響之下，我從小喜歡閱讀寫作是很自然的事。

教育與工作經驗（Education and Working Experiences）

Building up solid foundation of language abilities in English, I started doing related jobs. 建立了英文語言能力的穩固基礎後，我開始從事相關的工作。

興趣與技能（Interests and Skills）

Besides reading and writing, I worked hard to gain working skills concerning language capabilities. 除了閱讀和寫作，我努力取得語言能力相關的工作技能。

態度與期許（Attitudes and Expectations）

I'm so urged by the philosophy of self-development as to set up the goals of moving on in the working areas of telefilm translation. 我是如此地受到由自我發展理念的驅策，以致於訂定目標要在電視影片翻譯的工作領域更進一步。

▶ 圖解重點說明

關於應徵「電視影片翻譯員」英文自傳的書寫

重點：就文藝方面求職者而言，文學創作作品若曾有得獎的傑出表現，對應徵者是有加分的優勢。除了學歷、豐富打工經驗外，有實質的證照及電腦文書軟體使用技能，更增添獲得錄取工作的機會。

❶ 「**Under their influences, it is natural for me to love reading and writing since little.**」父母均是博學多聞的老師對應徵者寫文章的實力及靈感有所啟蒙。

❷ 「**Building up solid foundation of language abilities in English, I started doing related jobs.**」英文系主修及翻譯、口譯相關的打工經驗使應徵者更具有優質的條件。

❸ 「**Besides reading and writing, I worked hard to gain working skills concerning language capabilities.**」閱讀、寫作外，應徵者通過全民英檢，有能力使用電腦並具有勝任翻譯的技能。

❹ 「**I'm so urged by the philosophy of self-development as to set up the goals of moving on in the working areas of telefilm translation.**」自我期許甚高的應徵者，兼具興趣及能力，期盼為頗負盛名的翻譯社工作，拓展事業領域。

Part 1 句型篇

Part 2 圖解應用篇

141

英文自傳 便利貼光碟 1-5 Tips：實線和虛線是可以替換的地方，虛線同時也是單元重要句型，套色處結合 Part 1 句型文法的應用，整合式學習拓展寫作能力！

An Autobiography

My name is Cathy Yang, twenty-five years old. I'm the only child in the family. My parents are both Chinese teachers in senior high and are well-informed. Under their influences, it is natural for me to love reading and writing since little. To bathe myself in a world full of imagination and novelties always gives me great inspiration.

I majored in English in college. Building up solid foundation of language abilities in English, I started doing related jobs. I worked part time as an assistant editor for a local magazine, an interpreter in meetings and presentations. Above all, I enjoyed doing translation for TV channels.

Besides reading and writing, I worked hard to gain working skills concerning language capabilities. I obtained the Certificate of the High- intermediate Level of GEPT Test. I'm good at computer software, such as Windows, Powerpoint, Adobe PDF, etc. Also, I am capable of translating web-pages, cartoons, film and documentaries subtitling for TV channels.

I am careful, diligent, and enterprising. I'm so urged by the philosophy of self-development as to set up the goals of moving on in the working areas of telefilm translation. I expect to work for a prestigious translation agency like yours. If so, to be sure, I will obtain more professional experiences and further my interests and capabilities.

自傳

我是楊凱西，二十五歲。我是家中的獨生女，我的父母是高中的國文老師，兩人都博學多聞。在他們的影響之下，我從小喜歡閱讀寫作是很自然的事。沉浸於充滿想像及新奇的世界當中常常帶給我絕佳的靈感。

大學時我主修英語，建立了英文語言能力的穩固基礎後，我開始從事相關的工作。我兼差為地方雜誌做助理編輯，並且在會議及展場做口譯員，更重要的是我喜歡為電視頻道做翻譯的工作。

除了閱讀和寫作，我努力取得語言能力相關的工作技能。我通過了全民英檢中高級的測驗。我擅長使用電腦軟體，譬如 Windows、Powerpoint、Adobe PDF 等等。此外，我有能力翻譯網頁、卡通影片，並且為電視頻道的影片和紀錄片做字幕的翻譯。

我小心謹慎、勤勉，並且富進取心。我是如此地受到由自我發展理念的驅策，以致於訂定目標要在電視影片翻譯的工作領域更進一步。我期盼能進入像您這樣聲譽卓越的翻譯社裡工作。果真如此，可確定的是，我將得到更多專業的經驗，並且進一步發展我的興趣和潛能。

Part 1 句型篇

Part 2 圖解應用篇

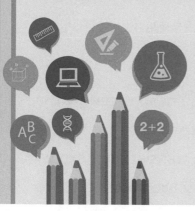

1-6
應徵「新聞記者」英文自傳
結合「新聞描述」句型應用
搭配文法：動名詞句型

▶ 圖解寫作架構

應徵職業（Applying Job）

A Journalist 新聞記者

家庭背景與影響（Family Background and Influences）

Thus, there is no surprising that, since young, I have determined to become a journalist. 於是，從小我立志要成為一名新聞記者也就不足為奇了。

教育與工作經驗（Education and Working Experiences）

I obtained basic knowledge and abundant experiences in newswork after becoming a Journalism major in college. 在大學主修新聞系後，我取得新聞方面的基本知識和豐富的經驗。

興趣與技能（Interests and Skills）

In addition to reading, writing, and web-browsing, I am fond of learning skills related to journalism. 除了閱讀、寫作，以及瀏覽網頁外，我喜歡學習與新聞相關的技能。

態度與期許（Attitudes and Expectations）

Being sociable, aggressive, and well-organized, I wish to make good use of my talent in journalism. 擅長社交、富有進取心，組織能力強的我希望能好好發揮我新聞方面的天份。

▶ 圖解重點說分明

關於應徵「新聞記者」英文自傳的書寫

重點：應徵者本身條件甚優，不僅是新聞系高材生，也有志朝此方面伸展抱負。自傳書寫中，可鉅細靡遺地敘述相關的經驗及技能、個人人格特質及對於未來前程的規劃及抱負，加深主試者的印象。

❶「**Thus, there is no surprising that, since young, I have determined to become a journalist.**」家人的鼓勵讓應徵者有志從事新聞工作，追求自我，探索世界。

❷「**I obtained basic knowledge and abundant experiences in newswork after becoming a Journalism major in college.**」學校社團及學生記者的歷練和學習增進應徵者擔任記者的能力。

❸「**In addition to reading, writing, and web-browsing, I am fond of learning skills related to journalism.**」閱讀廣泛、採訪文筆佳、電腦編輯能力強及細心足證應徵者有十足的專業能力。

❹「**Being sociable, aggressive, and well-organized, I wish to make good use of my talent in journalism.**」雖年輕，但有抱負、有實力，應徵者冀望接受更新更大的挑戰。

英文自傳 便利貼光碟 1-6 Tips：實線和虛線是可以替換的地方，虛線同時也是單元重要句型，套色處結合 Part 1 句型文法的應用，整合式學習拓展寫作能力！

An Autobiography

I am Linda Chou, aged twenty-three. My parents always advise me to explore new world fields and make self-improvements. Thus, there is no surprising that, since young, I have determined to become a journalist. I will explore the world and spread out information and ideas to the public.

I obtained basic knowledge and abundant experiences in newswork after becoming a Journalism major in college. In the school Club of Journalism, I gained skills of news editing and I realized the importance of teamwork and interpersonal skills. Besides, working as a student reporter in the campus enabled me to acquire a lot of practical news covering skills.

In addition to reading, writing, and web-browsing, I am fond of learning skills related to journalism. I have technical computer skills concerning news covering and editing. I can create and edit articles on major current events and interesting local stories. Besides, I am careful and cautious as to news reporting and editing with minimal mistakes.

Being sociable, aggressive, and well-organized, I wish to make good use of my talent in journalism. Though I am young, I am willing to learn and wish to be trusted with important and challenging news missions. I have a lot of confidence in my ability and my diligence. It goes without saying that I will do all out to complete the work assigned to me.

自傳

我是周琳達，二十三歲。我的父母一向建議我要探索新的世界領域，並且追求自我進步。於是，從小我立志要成為一名新聞記者也就不足為奇了。我將探索世界，並且傳遞資訊及理念給大眾。

在大學主修新聞系後，我取得新聞方面的基本知識和豐富的經驗。在學校的新聞社社團中，我學會了編輯新聞的技巧，而且我了解到團隊工作和人際關係的重要性。此外，在校園當學生記者使我得到許多實用的新聞採訪技術。

除了閱讀、寫作，以及瀏覽網頁外，我喜歡學習與新聞相關的技能。我懂得使用新聞採訪和編輯相關的軟體。我會撰寫及編輯重大時事和有趣的地方故事的文章。此外，我的細心和機警可以把新聞報導和編輯的錯誤降到最少。

擅長社交、富有進取心，組織能力強的我希望能好好發揮我新聞方面的天份。雖然我很年輕，但是我很願意學習並且希望能被賦予重要且富挑戰性的新聞任務。我對於我的能力和勤勉有很大的信心。我將會把指派給我的工作盡全力完成是自不待言的。

1-7
應徵「空服員」英文自傳
結合「綜合」句型應用
搭配文法：綜合應用句型

▶ **圖解寫作架構**

應徵職業（Applying Job）

A Flight Attendant 空服員

家庭背景與影響（Family Background and Influences）

Being used to taking care of others, I have become thoughtful and responsible. 由於習慣於照顧別人，我變得善解人意並且負責任感。

教育與工作經驗（Education and Working Experiences）

As a Foreign Languages major in college, I worked part time to expand my life circle. 身為大學外語系的學生，我打工兼差來拓展生活圈。

興趣與技能（Interests and Skills）

As I am interested in foreign cultures, I worked hard to master several different languages. 由於我對外國文化深感興趣，我努力精通數種不同的語言。

態度與期許（Attitudes and Expectations）

Demanding myself to pursue further knowledge and life experiences, I hope to enlarge the scope of life. 要求我自己追求更進一步的知識和生活經驗，我希望擴大生活圈。

▶ 圖解重點說分明

關於應徵「空服員」英文自傳的書寫

重點：應徵者有持續付出的精神，優異的多益測驗成績，流暢的外語能力，國際就學的經驗，及善於溝通、解決問題的能力等，優質的條件足以證明勝任工作的無限潛能。

❶「**Being used to taking care of others, I have become thoughtful and responsible.**」說明應徵者的家庭背景養成她關懷他人、負責任的態度。

❷「**As a Foreign Languages major in college, I worked part time to expand my life circle.**」此部份強調應徵者成績及外語能力佳，兼差的工作對象使她擅長於人際關係的處理。

❸「**As I am interested in foreign cultures, I worked hard to master several different languages.**」應徵者精通外語，具高EQ，溝通能力強。

❹「**Demanding myself to pursue further knowledge and life experiences, I hope to enlarge the scope of life.**」強調自身合宜的人格特質及深遠的自我期許，希望能求職成功。

英文自傳 便利貼光碟 1-7 Tips：實線和虛線是可以替換的地方，虛線同時也是單元重要句型！

An Autobiography

I am <u>Lily Wu</u>, <u>twenty-two</u> years of age. In my family, my parents are very busy. My father owns a trading company, and my mother is a nurse. As the eldest child, I usually have to look after my two little brothers. Being used to taking care of others, I have become thoughtful and responsible.

My scholastic performances have always been fine. In high school, I stayed in California for one year as an exchange student. As a Foreign Languages major in college, I worked part time to expand my life circle. I taught English in Children's English Center and assisted with affairs in my father's trading company when free. Thus, I have got familiar with people-oriented environment and become understanding and tolerant.

I enjoy traveling, making friends, and learning foreign languages. As I am interested in foreign cultures, I worked hard to master several different languages. I got 850 in TOEIC, and I can speak fluent English, Japanese and French. Furthermore, I have high EQ, and excellent interpersonal skills.

I am quite an enthusiastic and considerate person. Also, I am a creative problem-solver. Demanding myself to pursue further knowledge and life experiences, I hope to enlarge the scope of life. I wish I could have the chance to work in such a renowned airline as yours. I will try hard to be a competent flight attendant and carry out the tasks assigned to me.

自傳

我是吳莉莉，二十二歲。在我的家庭中，父母十分忙碌。爸爸開貿易公司，媽媽是護士。身為長女，我經常得照顧兩個年幼的弟弟。由於習慣於照顧別人，我變得善解人意並且負責任感。

我在校成績一向優良。高中時我以交換學生的身分在加州待了一年。身為大學外語系的學生，我打工兼差來拓展生活圈。閒暇時，我在兒童英語中心教英文，並且協助父親在貿易公司的工作。因此，我熟悉於與人相處的環境，並且變得具諒解和寬容之心。

我喜歡旅遊、交友，及學習外國語言。由於我對外國文化深感興趣，我努力精通數種不同的語言。我多益測驗得 850 分，而且我會說流利的英文、日文，及法文。再者，我有高 EQ，和絕佳的人際交往技巧。

我是一個十分熱忱及善解人意的人。此外，我也是一個很有創意的問題解決者。要求我自己追求更進一步的知識和生活經驗，我希望擴大生活圈。我期盼有機會在像您如此聲譽卓越的航空公司工作。我會盡力成為稱職的空服員，及執行指派給我的任務。

1-8
應徵「秘書」英文自傳
結合「綜合」句型應用
搭配文法：綜合應用句型

▶ 圖解寫作架構

應徵職業（Applying Job）

A Secretary 秘書

家庭背景與影響（Family Background and Influences）

Born and raised in a caring and loving family, I have a calming and positive temperament. 在充滿愛及關切的家庭中長大，我擁有沉穩和積極的個性。

教育與工作經驗（Education and Working Experiences）

I majored in Business Administration in college and worked as an office assistant in my department in senior year. 大學時我主修工商管理，大四時在系上擔任助教。

興趣與技能（Interests and Skills）

Taking great interest in languages and administration, I took extra night courses to increase my capabilities and skills. 由於對語言和管理有很大的興趣，我另外在晚上上課來增進我的能力和技術。

態度與期許（Attitudes and Expectations）

My great enthusiasm and proficient skills will enable me to be a competent secretary. 我高度的熱忱和純熟的技術將能促使我成為一名稱職的秘書。

▶ 圖解重點說分明

關於應徵「秘書」英文自傳的書寫

重點：應徵者學歷佳、助教應具的能力及工作內容與秘書工作類似，又肯增強自己多方面的能力，多益測驗成績十分優異，又善於組織和規劃。進取向上及全方位技能的特色是不可多得的好人才。

❶ 「**Born and raised in a caring and loving family, I have a calming and positive temperament.**」說明應徵者和樂的家庭背景對她沉穩、有條不紊的個性產生影響。

❷ 「**I majored in Business Administration in college and worked as an office assistant in my department in senior year.**」此部份強調應徵者不僅學有專長，大學中經由擔任助教所得的經驗亦訓練有成。

❸ 「**Taking great interest in languages and administration, I took extra night courses to increase my capabilities and skills.**」應徵者刻苦上進，增強她興趣濃厚語言及管理方面的能力，因而頗具專業技能。

❹ 「**My great enthusiasm and proficient skills will enable me to be a competent secretary.**」應徵者工作經驗不多，但有能力且有意願學習，應能勝任工作。

英文自傳 便利貼光碟 1-8 Tips：實線和虛線是可以替換的地方，虛線同時也是單元重要句型！

An Autobiography

I am Amy Wang, twenty-four year old. Born and raised in a caring and loving family, I have a calming and positive temperament. My father is an engineer, and my mother is a housewife. The atmosphere in our family is merry. We concern about each other and are happy to share everything.

I majored in Business Administration in college and worked as an office assistant in my department in senior year. I did well at my assistant work. I had strong administrative knowledge and excellent computer skills. As an efficient time-manager, I was detailed and precise in planning day to day schedule. What's more, I am good at data collection and management.

Taking great interest in languages and administration, I took extra night courses to increase my capabilities and skills. I got 800 in TOEIC, and I am well-trained for the secretarial position. Besides my proficient English ability, I am skilled in multiple computer applications. Also, with excellent organizational and planning skills, I can provide full secretarial support.

I am independent, well-organized, and trustworthy. My great enthusiasm and proficient skills will enable me to be a competent secretary. I've graduated from college for only a few months. Though I don't have too much work experience, I am keen and fast to learn. I believe, with my knowledge and specialty in secretarial work, I will make great contributions.

自傳

我是王愛美，二十四歲。在充滿愛及關切的家庭中長大，我擁有沉穩和積極的個性。我父親是工程師，母親是家庭主婦。家中的氣氛歡愉，我們彼此關心，並且樂於分享一切。

大學時我主修工商管理，大四時在系上擔任助教。我十分勝任於助教的工作。我有豐富的行政知識以及絕佳的電腦技能。身為有效率的時間管理者，我在規劃每日的進度上很細心且精準。再者，我擅長資料收集及處理。

由於對語言和管理有很大的興趣，我另外在晚上上課來增進我的能力和技術。我多益測驗得 800 分，就秘書工作來說，我訓練有素。除了我純熟的英文能力之外，我精通於多樣的電腦應用。此外，兼具有絕佳的組織和規劃的技能，我可以提供全面的祕書支援工作。

我十分獨立，組織能力強，並且值得信賴。我高度的熱忱和純熟的技術將能促使我成為一名稱職的秘書。我剛從大學畢業幾個月，雖然我並沒有太多的工作經驗，但是我熱衷學習而且學得很快。我相信，以我在祕書工作的知識和專長，我將會作出極大的貢獻。

1-9
應徵「電腦動畫師」英文自傳結合「綜合」句型應用
搭配文法：綜合應用句型

▶ 圖解寫作架構

應徵職業（Applying Job）
A Computer Animator 電腦動畫師

> **家庭背景與影響（Family Background and Influences）**
>
> My parents are thoughtful and responsible, which makes me one of the kind. 我的父母善解人意且負責任，而造就我具相同的個性。

> **教育與工作經驗（Education and Working Experiences）**
>
> While majoring in Animation Design & Game Programming, I took nighttime jobs as an assistant animation designer. 主修動畫與遊戲軟體設計之餘，我在夜間擔任助理動畫設計師。

> **興趣與技能（Interests and Skills）**
>
> Applying my interests of creating animated figures, I have acquired quite a few designing skills. 充分發揮我對於創造動畫人物的興趣，我具備相當多的設計技術。

> **態度與期許（Attitudes and Expectations）**
>
> I hold optimistic and responsible attitudes toward life, and I wish to make use of my artistic talent. 我對人生充滿樂觀及負責任的態度，我希望能充分發揮我的藝術天分。

圖解重點說分明

關於應徵「電腦動畫師」英文自傳的書寫

重點：應徵者的濃厚興趣與優質技能相輔相成。細心、具創意、積極上進的人格特質也是可取的優點。附上個人作品網頁的連結，專業能力強，是吸引雇主的一大特色，條件佳，謀職成功機率則高。

❶「**My parents are thoughtful and responsible, which makes me one of the kind.**」說明應徵者的家庭小康，父母關愛負責，使他亦具同樣的特質。

❷「**While majoring in Animation Design & Game Programming, I took nighttime jobs as an assistant animation designer.**」應徵者由對漫畫的興趣引伸出大學就讀與動畫設計相關的科系，全心投入學習，並在夜間兼做助理設計師。

❸「**Applying my interests of creating animated figures, I have acquired quite a few designing skills.**」興趣與技能兩者的結合外加團隊合作的態度，造就應徵者的好條件。

❹「**I hold optimistic and responsible attitudes toward life, and I wish to make use of my artistic talent.**」積極態度與發揮才華的期許作為結論，企盼能開拓新的境界。

英文自傳 便利貼光碟 1-9 Tips：實線和虛線是可以替換的地方，虛線同時也是單元重要句型！

An Autobiography

I am Mason Hu, aged twenty-five. I come from a middle-class family. There are four members in my family: my parents, my younger brother, and me. My parents are both blue collar workers; my brother, a student. My parents are thoughtful and responsible, which makes me one of the kind.

Since little, I have liked watching cartoons, reading comic strips, and drawing characters. While majoring in Animation Design & Game Programming, I took nighttime jobs as an assistant animation designer. Since I am a big fan of the comic books of superhero-themed serials, I focused on exploring techniques of designing animations for characters.

I love watching dazzling animated films full of visual imagery, and I never get tired of working on computer animation. Applying my interests of creating animated figures, I have acquired quite a few designing skills. I can creatively design animated characters, proficiently use the technical illustrating tools, and collaborate well with my teammates.

Besides great attention to detail, I am patient, persistent, and reliable. I hold optimistic and responsible attitudes toward life, and I wish to make use of my artistic talent. Expecting to work further on 3D computer animation, I will make every effort to do the new job well. (For a sample of my animation portfolio, visit http://youtu.be/WpyfrixBdA on YouTube.)

自傳

我是胡梅森，二十五歲。我來自於中產家庭，家中有四名成員：雙親、弟弟和我。我的父母皆為藍領階級；我弟弟是學生。我的父母善解人意且負責任，而造就我具相同的個性。

從小，我一向喜歡看卡通、閱讀漫畫，並且畫漫畫人物。主修動畫與遊戲軟體設計之餘，我在夜間擔任助理動畫設計師。由於我是英雄主題系列漫畫的粉絲，我專心探索設計人物動畫的技術。

我喜歡看充滿視覺意象炫目的動畫影片，而且我絕對不會厭倦於電腦動畫的工作。充分發揮我對於創造動畫人物的興趣，我具備相當多的設計技術。我會很有創意地設計動畫角色，純熟地使用電腦繪畫工具，並且和我的隊友合作無間。

除了注意細節的特點之外，我非常有耐心、恆心，而且很可靠。我對人生充滿樂觀及負責任的態度，我希望能充分發揮我的藝術天分。我期盼在 3D 電腦動畫上有近一步的發展，我將會努力把新的工作做好。

（請上 YouTube 網站：http://youtu.be/WpyfrixBdA 觀看參考我動畫作品選輯。）

Part 1 句型篇

Part 2 圖解應用篇

1-10

英文自傳結合生活描述
句型應用小練習

▶ **英文自傳結合生活事件描述小回顧**

　　中標社會新鮮人求職自傳可依描述應徵者的「家庭背景與影響」，「教育與工作經驗」，「興趣與技能」，以及「態度與期許」四大方面對自己做介紹。由於大學剛畢業不久或剛退伍，欠缺專職的工作經驗，所以，大學在校的好成績，科系所得基本專業知識，熱心公益社區義工的服務以及學校社團的表現學習以外，可多介紹打工兼職時取得的工作心得及技能，以取得主管或雇主的好印象。若有語言、技能證照，或作品集置於網站上供人瀏覽以印證能力及潛力則更佳。總而言之，自傳中要能傳達自己健康、樂觀的人生觀，專業的技能、優點、潛力，肯學習的積極態度，和很高的自我期許要求，好讓主試者感受到極富價值、又具可塑性的你就是他們要尋找最適當的人選。

▶ 文法句型補一補

( ) 1. Steven often _____ vacations to Hawaii and Australia.

(A) takes   (B) took   (C) taking   (D) will take

( ) 2. Nowadays, people who work at home _____ SOHO.

(A) is called   (B) call

(C) are called   (D) will call

( ) 3. _____ is popular to chat on Line with friends by Smartphone.

(A) to   (B) This   (C) It   (D) That

( ) 4. Jane _____ the credit card to pay for her purchases in the shopping mall yesterday.

(A) used   (B) using   (C) use   (D) uses

( ) 5. With so many movies on cable TV channels, we _____ always find a good film to watch.

(A) must not   (B) can   (C) should   (D) can't

( ) 6. Edward enjoys _____ Harry Potter because of its mysterious magic world.

(A) read   (B) to read   (C) reads   (D) reading

Part 1 句型篇

Part 2 圖解應用篇

161

答案與解析

1. (A) took

題目中譯 史帝芬時常到夏威夷和澳洲度假。

答案解析 時間副詞 often 意指平時常有例行的習慣動作，常搭配現在式，主詞 Steven 是第三人稱單數，一般動詞 take 字尾要加 s，故應選 (A)。

2. (C) are called

題目中譯 今日來說，在家中工作的人被稱為蘇活族。

答案解析 nowadays 表示今日的狀態，用現在式。被稱呼為…，要用被動語態 be V + pp，故應選 (C) are called。

3. (C) It

題目中譯 經由手機使用 Line 和朋友聊天是很普遍的。

答案解析 不定詞放在句首做主詞用過長時，用假主詞 it 取代，真正不定詞則放在句尾。故應選 (C) It。

4. (A) used

題目中譯 珍昨天使用信用卡來支付她在賣場所購買的物品。

答案解析 yesterday 指昨天，過去的時間，要搭配過去式。故選 (A) used。

5. (B) can

題目中譯 有線電視頻道上有如此多的電影，我們總是可以找到好的影片來觀賞。

答案解析 有許多電視影片可供我們選擇，合乎語意邏輯的情態助動詞以 (B) 選項 can 為佳，故應選 (B)。

6. ⒟ reading

題目中譯 艾德華喜歡閱讀《哈利波特》是由於書中神秘的魔幻世界。

答案解析 及物動詞後，要接受詞。及物動詞 enjoy 在句中要接動名詞 reading 做為受詞。故應選 (D)。

▶ 寫作老師巧巧說

應徵工作時，中文自傳外，英文自傳的增列可提升國際化的好印象，增加錄取機會。在寫作時要注意誠懇實在，宜避免浮誇不實。英文拼字、時態、文法、句子錯誤儘量減少，以免弄巧成拙。自傳的書寫要簡潔扼要，確實精準，用字遣詞要能達意，內容言之有物，可有加分效果，求職必將順利成功。

2-1
英文報告「與眾不同的好萊塢新興女星：珍妮佛‧羅倫斯」結合「人事物描述」句型應用

搭配文法：虛詞 it 及 there 句型

▶ **圖解寫作架構**

> **Jennifer Lawrence**
> 珍妮佛‧勞倫斯

Background（背景）

Jennifer Lawrence is a famous American actress, born on August 15, 1990, Kentucky. 珍妮佛‧勞倫斯是著名的美國女演員，1990 年 8 月 15 日誕生於肯塔基州。

Achievements（成就）

Jennifer has achieved amazing success in her movie career. 珍妮佛在她的電影事業締造驚人的成就。

Characteristics（特色）

Owing to her great charm and good deeds, Jennifer has received worldwide popularity. 珍妮佛以她迷人的魅力和良好的事蹟，廣受全世界的歡迎。

Future Prospects（未來展望）

Besides filming, she is determined to become an outstanding director. 拍戲之外，她下定決心要成為一名傑出的導演。

▶ 圖解重點說分明

關於英文報告「與眾不同的好萊塢新興女星：珍妮佛‧勞倫斯」的講稿書寫

重點：「人事物描述」英文報告主要可由描述主角人物的「Background（背景）」，「Achievements（成就）」，「Characteristics（特色）」，以及「Future Prospects（未來展望）」四大方面做完整而且令人印象深刻的介紹。

❶「**Jennifer Lawrence is a famous American actress, born on August 15, 1990, Kentucky.**」說明美國著名女演員，珍妮佛‧勞倫斯的出生背景以及成名的經過。

❷「**Jennifer has achieved amazing success in her movie career.**」敘述珍妮佛在電影事業方面的發展及成就。她甚至以 22 歲，有史以來第二年輕的年紀，獲頒奧斯卡最佳女主角獎。

❸「**Owing to her great charm and good deeds, Jennifer has received worldwide popularity.**」描述珍妮佛如何以她迷人的人格特質、勇氣，及慷慨獲得世人的喜愛。

❹「**Besides filming, she is determined to become an outstanding director.**」最後預期以她的決心和勤勉，她想成為導演的夢想必將能實現作為結論。

英文範文

英文講稿 便利貼光碟 2-1 Tips：套色處是可以替換的地方！虛線是重要句型！

An Extraordinary New Hollywood Actress: Jennifer Lawrence

Hi! It's my pleasure to introduce you Jennifer Lawrence. Jennifer Lawrence is a famous American actress, born on August 15, 1990, Kentucky. Since little, she has loved to perform by dressing up as a clown or ballerina. At 14, she was spotted and started her acting career.

There is no denying that Jennifer has achieved amazing success in her movie career. Her excellent performing skills brought her great fame. The role in *The Hunger Games* In 2012 won her recognition as a real star. And her reputation reached culmination when in 2013, aged only 22, she won Oscar Award for Best Actress in *Silver Linings Playbook*.

Now, it is time to show you the next slide. Owing to her great charm and good deeds, Jennifer has received worldwide popularity. She is beautiful, hilarious, and talented. Besides, what attracts the world is her courage to voice for women's rights and her generosity to offer charitable support.

It's reported that Jennifer is now making more films. Besides filming, she is determined to become an outstanding director. In conclusion, there is no doubt that with her strong will and hard work, she will soon realize her dream. Thank you for your attention!

與眾不同的好萊塢新興女星：珍妮佛・羅倫斯

嗨！很榮幸為各位介紹：珍妮佛・羅倫斯。珍妮佛・羅倫斯是著名的美國女演員，1990 年 8 月 15 日誕生於肯塔基州。從小，珍妮佛喜愛打扮成小丑或芭蕾舞者。14 歲時被發掘而開始她的演藝生涯。

無可否認，珍妮佛在她的電影事業締造驚人的成就，她優異的演技使她聲名大噪。2012 年《飢餓遊戲》中的角色確立她巨星的地位。她的聲望在 2013 年到達最高峰，以只有 22 歲的年齡藉由《派特的幸福劇本》獲頒奧斯卡最佳女主角獎。

現在為各位播放下一張幻燈片。珍妮佛以她迷人的魅力和良好的事蹟，廣受全世界的歡迎。她美麗、風趣，而且才華洋溢。此外，真正吸引世人的是她為婦女權益發聲的勇氣以及提供慈善援助的慷慨。

據報導，珍妮佛目前在拍攝更多影片。拍戲之外，她下定決心要成為一名傑出的導演。總之，無庸置疑地，以她堅強的意志及勤奮不懈的精神，她必將很快地實現她的夢想。感謝各位專注的聆聽！

2-2
英文報告「賴瑞・佩奇，謝爾蓋・布林與他們傑出的發明：谷歌」結合「人事物描述」句型應用

搭配文法：祈使句句型

▶ **圖解寫作架構**

Larry Page and Sergy Brin
賴瑞・佩奇與謝爾蓋・布林

Background（背景）
It was Larry Page and Sergy Brin who invented it. 它是由賴瑞・佩奇以及謝爾蓋・布林所發明的。

Achievements（成就）
And, it has become a technology company specializing in Internet-related services and products. 於是它成為一間專門提供與網際網路相關的服務及產品的科技公司。

Characteristics（特色）
Page and Brin are innovative, enterprising and forward-looking. 佩奇和布林兩人非常具創意、進取心，以及前瞻性。

Future Prospects（未來展望）
The world's information will be put on the Internet, universally accessible and useful. 全世界的資訊將會被放置在網際網路上，提供全球方便的使用途徑。

▶ 圖解重點說分明

關於英文報告「賴瑞‧佩奇，謝爾蓋‧布林與他們傑出的發明：谷歌」的講稿書寫

重點：「人事物描述」時，在開場白、中間串場，及結束作結論方面皆可利用祈使句句型讓聽眾注意報告的人物及相關主題。由描述主要人物的「Background（背景）」介紹影響主要人物的起源細節。

❶ 「**It was Larry Page and Sergy Brin who invented it.**」說明美國大學生賴瑞‧佩奇與謝爾蓋‧布林具共通興趣及想法而相識的經過。

❷ 「**And, it has become a technology company specializing in Internet-related services and products.**」敘述兩人共同努力籌錢而成功地創立提供與網際網路相關的服務及產品的谷歌公司。

❸ 「**Page and Brin are innovative, enterprising and forward-looking.**」描述兩人非常具創意、進取心，以及前瞻性，他們努力實現理想，終於成功。

❹ 「**The world's information will be put on the Internet, universally accessible and useful.**」最後以預期兩人將會提供全球網際網路資訊方便的使用途徑而帶來更多的貢獻作為結論。

Part 1 句型篇

Part 2 圖解應用篇

英文講稿 便利貼光碟 2-2 Tips：套色處是可以替換的地方！虛線是重要句型！

Larry Page, Sergy Brin and their Brilliant Invention, Google

Hello! Look at this slide. This is Google. It was Larry Page and Sergy Brin who invented it. They first met in 1995 at Stanford University. They shared the common interests in computers and the amazing invention was thus made.

Let me explain, and you will understand better. In 1996, they decided to create a better and faster search engine. With their maxed credit cards, they worked hard on raising money. After great efforts, in 1998, they founded Google. And, it has become a technology company specializing in Internet-related services and products.

As we all know, "Go on working, or nothing can be achieved." Page and Brin are innovative, enterprising and forward-looking. They tried hard to put their ideals into practice. Despite difficulties, they stuck to their dreams. Finally, their persistence paid off, and their great invention changed the world.

Page and Brin now respectively work as CEO and president

and are making further contributions. The world's information will be put on the Internet, universally accessible and useful. Allow me to conclude here: So, they actually "Do the right thing," as their company motto phrases it. Thanks!

賴瑞‧佩奇，謝爾蓋‧布林與他們傑出的發明，谷歌

嗨！請看這張幻燈片。這是谷歌。它是由賴瑞‧佩奇以及謝爾蓋‧布林發明。他們 1995 年於史丹佛大學初次認識。他們對於電腦有共同的興趣，驚人的發明就此誕生。

由我來解說，各位會比較瞭解。1996 年，他們決定要發明一個較好且較快速的搜尋引擎。帶著刷爆的信用卡，他們致力於籌募資金。經歷一番努力後，他們於 1998 年創立了谷歌。於是它成為一間專門提供與網際網路相關的服務及產品的科技公司。

正如大家所知，「要持續奮戰，否則終將一事無成。」佩奇和布林兩人非常具創意、進取心，以及前瞻性，他們努力將理想付諸實現。儘管遭逢困難，他們固守夢想。最後，他們的堅持有了回報，他們偉大的發明改變了全世界。

佩奇和布林現在分別擔任執行長和總裁，正在做出更多的貢獻。全世界的資訊將會被放置在網際網路上，提供全球方便的使用途徑。容我來結論：因此，正如他們公司座右銘所言，他們確實是在"做正確的事"。謝謝！

2-3
英文報告「首位非裔美籍總統：巴拉克·歐巴馬的成就」結合「人事物描述」句型應用

搭配文法：名詞子句句型

▶ **圖解寫作架構**

Barack Obama
巴拉克·歐巴馬

Background（背景）

He made history when becoming the 44th and the first African-American US President in 2008. 他在 2008 年成為美國第 44 屆總統，並且以首位非裔美籍總統的身分創造歷史。

Achievements in Domestic Affairs（內政的成就）

During the two terms, Obama, in spite of the fact that he met with critical challenges and oppositions, he still made great achievements. 在兩任的任期內，儘管面臨嚴苛的挑戰和反對，歐巴馬仍舊締造偉大的成就。

Achievements in Foreign Affairs（外交的成就）

In foreign affairs, Obama ended the war in Iraq, stood strong against ISIS, and continued America's leadership on global climate change. 就外交而言，歐巴馬終結伊拉克戰爭、強烈對抗 ISIS，以及持續美國在全球氣候變遷領導者的地位。

Characteristics（特色）

Obama has his special charisma of righteousness, resolution, and leadership. 歐巴馬具備了正義、堅決，和領袖的特質。

▶ 圖解重點說分明

關於英文報告「首位非裔美籍總統：巴拉克・歐巴馬的成就」的講稿書寫

重點：「人事物描述」英文報告時，可利用名詞子句的句型引領出報告人物相關的重點內容。本文由描述歐巴馬總統具體內政及外交上的成就彰顯他吸引民心的人格特質及居於世界領袖的出眾才華。

❶「He made history when becoming the 44ᵗʰ and the first African-American US President in 2008.」說明歐巴馬總統以首位美國非裔美籍總統的身分創造歷史的背景以及連任的經過。

❷「During the two terms, Obama, in spite of the fact that he met with critical challenges and oppositions, he still made great achievements.」敘述歐巴馬總統不屈不撓，在內政上卓越的成就。

❸「In foreign affairs, Obama ended the war in Iraq, stood strong against ISIS, and continued America's leadership on global climate change.」描述歐巴馬總統在外交上也締造的傑出貢獻。

❹「Obama has his special charisma of righteousness, resolution, and leadership.」最後以歐巴馬正義、堅決的特質以及吸引民心、激勵人心的說服力以及非凡的意志力而充分勝任總統職責作為結論。

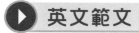
英文講稿 便利貼光碟 2-3 Tips：套色處是可以替換的地方！虛線是重要句型！

Achievements of the First African-American President:
Barack Obama

Hi. President Obama has always hoped that through his strong will, he could change America. He made history when becoming the 44th and the first African-American US President in 2008. In 2012, he was reelected to fulfill his guarantee that he would move the greatest nation on earth forward.

During the two terms, Obama, in spite of the fact that he met with critical challenges and oppositions, he still made great achievements. In domestic affairs, he boosted economy, lowered unemployment rate, and expanded health insurance coverage. Also, he created public well-being, enforced strict gun-control, supported legal same-sex marriage, and so on.

In foreign affairs, Obama ended the war in Iraq, stood strong against ISIS, and continued America's leadership on global climate change. Also, he fortified the trans-pacific partnership, reestablished diplomatic relations with Cuba, promoted world peace, and more. It turned out that in 2009, he was honorably awarded the Nobel Peace Prize.

<u>Obama has his special charisma of righteousness, resolution, and leadership.</u> What attracts the public most is his remarkable will. He successfully proves that when Americans are united as one, nothing cannot be done, for, they all hold the same creed: Yes, we can! Thanks!

首位非裔美籍總統：巴拉克・歐巴馬的成就

歐巴馬總統一向希望能經由他堅強的意志改變美國。他在 2008 年成為美國第 44 屆總統，並且以首位非裔美籍總統的身分創造歷史。在 2012 年，他連任以實現他將引領世上最偉大的國家向前邁進的承諾。

在兩任的任期內，儘管面臨嚴苛的挑戰和反對，歐巴馬仍舊締造偉大的成就。內政方面，他振興經濟、降低失業率，並擴大健保範圍。此外，他替公眾創造福利、嚴格加強槍枝管制，以及支持同性婚姻合法化等等。

就外交而言，歐巴馬終結伊拉克戰爭、強烈對抗 ISIS，以及持續美國在全球氣候變遷領導者的地位。此外，他鞏固環太平洋的夥伴關係、重建與古巴的外交關係，和促進世界和平等等。結果在 2009 年，他光榮地獲頒諾貝爾和平獎。

歐巴馬具備了正義、堅決，和領袖的特質。他最吸引大眾的是他非凡的意志力。他成功地證明，當美國人團結一致時，凡事皆能無往不利，因為他們持有相同的信念：是的，我們一定辦的到！謝謝！

2-4
英文報告「日本動畫大師：宮崎駿」結合「人事物描述」句型應用

搭配文法：假設語氣句型

 **圖解寫作架構**

Hayao Miyazaki
宮崎駿

Background（背景）

With the fondness of classical Japanese animation, Miyazaki has always wished that he could dedicate himself to animation. 由於對日本古典動畫的喜愛，宮崎駿一向期許自己可以致力於動畫創作。

Achievements（成就）

Miyazaki's animation enjoyed great popularity in Japan and across the globe. 宮崎駿的動畫在日本及國外都深受歡迎。

Characteristics（特色）

The themes and characters in his works make him unique and praiseworthy. 他作品中的主題和人物促使他成為獨特且值得讚揚的導演。

Future Prospects（未來展望）

Though in 2013, Miyazaki announced his retirement; fortunately, he's turned to creating CGI animated short films recently. 雖然在 2013 年，宮崎駿宣布退休；幸好，他最近轉向從事電腦動畫短片的創造。

▶ 圖解重點說分明

關於英文報告「日本動畫大師：宮崎駿」的講稿書寫

重點：「人事物描述」英文報告時，可利用假設語氣的句型引領出報告人物相關的重點內容。本文由描述日本大師，宮崎駿在動畫中提升人類自我學習成長的主題以及和地球共存的責任意識上的提倡及成就促使他成為世界級的動畫導演。

❶「**With the fondness of classic Japanese animation, Miyazaki has always wished that he could dedicate himself to animation.**」說明日本動畫大師，宮崎駿早期就才華洋溢，備受矚目的背景以及成名的經過。

❷「**Miyazaki's animation enjoyed great popularity in Japan and across the globe.**」敘述宮崎駿的動畫作品在日本國內享有盛名後，擴及到國外而終獲奧斯卡金像獎以及國際盛讚的經過。

❸「**The themes and characters in his works make him unique and praiseworthy.**」描述宮崎駿動畫作品的主題和人物促使他成為獨特且值得讚揚的導演並獲得世人的敬重及喜愛。

❹「**Though in 2013, Miyazaki announced his retirement; fortunately, he's turned to creating CGI animated short films recently.**」最後以鼓勵大家到東京欣賞大師近期以高科技製作的絕佳新作為結論。

英文講稿 便利貼光碟 2-4 Tips：套色處是可以替換的地方！虛線是重要句型！

The Japanese Master of Animation: Hayao Miyazaki

If you're familiar with animators, you can identify Hayao Miyazaki. With the fondness of classical Japanese animation, Miyazaki has always wished that he could dedicate himself to animation. Starting his career in 1963, he soon drew attention with his fantastic drawing and endless movie ideas.

Miyazaki's animation enjoyed great popularity in Japan and across the globe. His special hand-drawn works became well-known in Japan. Besides, without Walt Disney Company's efforts, his works would not have been appreciated abroad. In 2001, the film, *Spirited Away*, won him the Academy Award and international acclaims.

The themes and characters in his works make him unique and praiseworthy. Through his characters, the universal themes of humans fighting and choosing between good and evil to learn and grow are revealed. With strong sense of social responsibility, he rejects human violence and pollution, and he emphasizes harmony, nature, and ecology.

Though in 2013, Miyazaki announced his retirement; fortunately, he's turned to creating CGI animated short films recently. Therefore, I strongly recommend that you visit his Studio Ghibli Museum in Tokyo to appreciate his newly-made works filled with high technology. Take my advice.

日本動畫大師：宮崎駿

假使你熟悉動畫設計師，你可以認出這是宮崎駿。由於對日本古典動畫的喜愛，宮崎駿一向期許自己可以致力於動畫創作。1963 年創業後，他以絕妙的繪畫技術和無止盡的電影點子受到矚目。

宮崎駿的動畫在日本及國外都深受歡迎。他特殊的手繪動畫在日本頗負盛名。此外，若非有迪士尼動畫公司的幫助，他的作品在國外將可能不會被欣賞到。2001 年，《神隱少女》讓他獲頒美國奧斯卡金像獎以及國際的讚譽。

他作品中的主題和人物促使他成為獨特且值得讚揚的導演。他的人物呈現人類奮鬥及在是與非間作抉擇而學習成長的主題。帶有強烈的社會責任感，他反對人類的暴力和汙染，他重視和諧、大自然，及生態。

雖然在 2013 年，宮崎駿宣布退休；幸好，他最近轉向從事電腦動畫短片的創造。因此，我強力推薦您到東京參觀他的吉卜利動畫博物館欣賞他利用高科技所製作的絕佳新作，請接受我的建議。

2-5
英文報告「林書豪：帶來林來瘋的哈佛小子」結合「人事物描述」句型應用

搭配文法：轉承副詞句型

圖解寫作架構

> **Jeremy Lin**
> 林書豪

>> **Background（背景）**
>> Born on August 23, 1988, Ca., Lin is a second-generation Asian American and a Harvard graduate. 1988 年 8 月 23 日在加州誕生的林書豪是二代華裔美國人，哈佛畢業生。

>> **Achievements（成就）**
>> Through Linsanity, Asian Americans' achievements impressed the world. 透過林來瘋，亞裔美國人的成就令世人刮目相看。

>> **Characteristics（特色）**
>> In fact, it was his marvelous skills and humble response to Linsanity that appealed to fans around the world. 事實上，是他精湛的球技以及對於林來瘋謙虛的回應吸引了全世界眾多的球迷。

>> **Future Prospects（未來展望）**
>> Lin signed with Brooklyn Nets, and will definitely present the world with more outstanding basketball-playing and inspiration-creating. 林書豪與布魯克林籃網隊簽約打新的球季，他一定會呈現給世人更多精湛的球技以及鼓舞的力量。

▶ 圖解重點說明

關於英文報告「林書豪：帶來林來瘋的哈佛小子」的講稿書寫重點：利用轉承副詞的句型可引領出一氣呵成、行文流暢的報告。本文描述華裔美國人哈佛小子林書豪，以優異球技帶來「林來瘋」，一夕成名的經過，及亞裔人士的謙卑、信仰，和成就。

❶「**Born on August 23, 1988, Ca., Lin is a second-generation Asian American and a Harvard graduate.**」說明 NBA 球星林書豪學歷好、球技精湛，但一直未能順遂得意的情境。

❷「**Through Linsanity, Asian Americans' achievements impressed the world.**」敘述林書豪以優異球技帶來「林來瘋」，成為家喻戶曉球星的經過，及亞裔美國人的成就令世人刮目相看的榮耀。

❸「**In fact, it was his marvelous skills and humble response to Linsanity that appealed to fans around the world.**」描述林書豪的球技、謙遜，及信仰堅貞的特質獲得全世界球迷的仰慕及喜愛。

❹「**Lin signed with Brooklyn Nets, and will definitely present the world with more outstanding basketball-playing and inspiration-creating.**」最後以林書豪將會為世人打更多精采的好球並以他良好的謙虛風範鼓舞大眾作為結論。

181

英文講稿 便利貼光碟 2-5 Tips：套色處是可以替換的地方！虛線是重要句型！

Jeremy Lin: The Harvard Kid that Brought Linsanity

Hi! This is NBA star, Jeremy Lin. Born on August 23, 1988, Ca., Lin is a second-generation Asian American and a Harvard graduate. He played school teams all the way with superb performances. However, entering NBA afterwards brought him neither much good luck nor big fame.

It wasn't until 2012 when he made the world go Lin-sane. Scoring 171 points, he led the Nicks to a 7-game winning streak. Fans were fascinated by his versatility, and therefore, he became famous. Though racial stereotypes often deterred his career, he emerged as an inspiration. Through Linsanity, Asian Americans' achievements impressed the world.

In fact, it was his marvelous skills and humble response to Linsanity that appealed to fans around the world. In addition, his Christian faith plays a key role in his popularity. With belief, he never loses confidence in himself. In short, playing basketball well is his primary job all for the glory of the God.

Thus, from an unknown athlete to a renowned NBA star,

Lin proves that with determination, achieving a dream is no impossible task. Now, Lin signed with Brooklyn Nets, and will definitely present the world with more outstanding basketball-playing and inspiration-creating. Thanks!

林書豪：帶來林來瘋的哈佛小子

嗨！這位是 NBA 球星，林書豪。1988 年 8 月 23 日在加州誕生的林書豪是二代華裔美國人，哈佛畢業生。他一路以卓越的表現打校隊。然而，後來加入 NBA 未替他帶來太多的好運，也未帶來盛名。

直到 2012 年，他使全世界為之瘋狂。他得到 171 分，帶領尼克隊贏得 7 場連勝。球迷為他的多才多藝著迷，他因此成名。雖然種族刻板印象常阻礙他的事業，他成為一股鼓舞力量。透過林來瘋，亞裔美國人的成就令世人刮目相看。

事實上，是他精湛的球技以及對於林來瘋謙虛的回應吸引了全世界眾多的球迷。此外，他的基督信仰是他受歡迎的關鍵。內心存有信念，他從不喪失自信。簡言之，把籃球打好是他的首要工作，目的是要光耀上帝。

由此，從默默無名的運動員到知名的 NBA 球星，林書豪證實只要有決心，實現夢想並非無法達成的任務。目前林書豪與布魯克林籃網隊簽約打新的球季，他一定會呈現給世人更多精湛的球技以及鼓舞的力量。謝謝！

英文報告「我最欽佩的人：我的母親」結合「人事物描述」句型應用

搭配文法：連接詞句型

▶ 圖解寫作架構

My Mother
我的母親

Background（背景）

I'm here to talk about my dear mother, who is also the person I admire most. 在此我要談論我最親愛的母親，同時也是我最欽佩的人。

Achievements（成就）

She is so talented and marvelous! 她是位如此有天分、了不起的人物！

Characteristics（特色）

Kind and easy-going in the appearance as she is, she is strict with us children. 雖然外表上仁慈而且平易近人，她對我們這些孩子是很嚴格的。

Future Prospects（未來展望）

To be brief, my respectable mother has a great influence on my conduct and character. 總而言之，我值得敬重的媽媽對於我的行為和人格有著重大的影響。

▶ 圖解重點說分明

關於英文報告「我最欽佩的人：我的母親」的講稿書寫

重點：「人事物描述」英文報告時，對等及附屬連接詞句型的運用可使人物報告精簡扼要，內容有物。本文描述作者的母親成為他最欽佩的人的因素，並表達對母親永遠的感念及敬愛。

❶「**I'm here to talk about my dear mother, who is also the person I admire most.**」母親節即將來臨，作者在報告中闡述母親的特殊之處，及敬愛崇拜母親的深情。

❷「**She is so talented and marvelous!**」敘述母親待人謙恭、敬業行事、認真稱職，及善於烹調、園藝等令人讚嘆的特質。

❸「**Kind and easy-going in the appearance as she is, she is strict with us children.**」描述媽媽寵愛但不溺愛孩子的原則，及個性隨和、關懷他人的態度，堪稱是位模範母親。

❹「**To be brief, my respectable mother has a great influence on my conduct and character.**」最後感謝母親樹立的典範及影響，並虔誠真摯地祝福媽媽：母親節快樂！

英文講稿 便利貼光碟 2-6 Tips：套色處是可以替換的地方！虛線是重要句型！

The Person I Admire Most: My Mother

Hello! The tradition of honoring mothers on Mother's Day is great. Since the holiday is coming, I'm here to talk about my dear mother, who is also the person I admire most.

My mom, 45 years old, is quiet and elegant-looking. As a librarian, she is not only efficient and responsible at work but kind and friendly to everyone. As soon as she gets back home, she dedicates herself to the family. She's especially good at cooking and baking cakes. What's more, she has such green fingers as to grow beautiful plants. She is so talented and marvelous!

Kind and easy-going in the appearance as she is, she is strict with us children. She emphasizes character-building and teaches us how to tell right from wrong. She demands us to study hard and become well-informed. Besides, she often reads and exchanges opinions with us. She's liberal in accepting others' ideas and has set us a good example.

To be brief, my respectable mother has a great influence

on my conduct and character. I'm lucky to have such a great mother. Finally, I'd like to say to my beloved mother, "Happy Mother's Day!" Thank you!

我最欽佩的人：我的母親

大家好！正如大家所知，在母親節表示對媽媽尊敬的傳統是很棒的。由於母親節即將來臨，在此我要談論我最親愛的母親，同時也是我最欽佩的人。

我的媽媽，四十五歲，外表文靜且高雅。身為圖書管理員，她工作上不僅有效率、負責任，待人也十分仁慈和善。一回到家，她致力於照顧家人。她尤其擅長於烹飪及烘焙蛋糕。此外，她如此地精通園藝以致於可以種植出美麗的植物。她是如此有天分、了不起的人物！

雖然外表上仁慈而且平易近人，她對我們這些孩子是很嚴格的。她重視人格的培養，並教導我們如何分辨是非。她要求我們努力用功並增廣見聞。再者，她時常閱讀，和我們交換意見。她思想開放，能夠接受他人想法，並且為我們樹立良好的典範。

總之，我值得敬重的媽媽對於我的行為和人格有著重大的影響。我很幸運能夠擁有如此偉大的媽媽。最後，我想要跟我親愛的媽媽說："母親節快樂！"謝謝！

2-7
英文報告「歐普拉・溫芙蕾和她的脫口秀」結合「人事物描述」句型應用

搭配文法：綜合應用句型

▶ **圖解寫作架構**

Oprah Winfrey
歐普拉・溫芙蕾

Background（背景）

Born in 1954, Winfrey had a troubled adolescence; however, after she started living with her father, things changed. 誕生於 1954 年，歐普拉有一段令她困擾的青少年時期；然而，自從開始和父親一起生活後，事情有所改觀了。

Achievements（成就）

Among the outstanding achievements, the high view-rating Oprah Winfrey Show she hosted won great fame and popularity. 在眾多傑出的成就中，她所主持的高收率節目《歐普拉脫口秀》廣受好評。

Characteristics（特色）

Winfrey has attracted nationwide popularity because of her talent, passion, and persuasiveness. 由於歐普拉的才華、熱情，和她擅長說服人的特質受到全國的歡迎。

Future Prospects（未來展望）

Oprah still humbly considers herself an ordinary person and is fully devoted to her network and charitable affairs. 歐普拉依舊謙虛地認為自己是個平凡人，並且全力致力於廣播網和慈善事業。

▶ 圖解重點說分明

關於英文報告「歐普拉‧溫芙蕾和她的脫口秀」的講稿書寫

重點：英文報告使用的句型可增添變化，措辭簡易口語，藉以吸引在場聽眾全程的注意，做出成功的報告。本文描述美國最具有影響力和最富有的女黑人媒體名人，歐普拉‧溫芙蕾成名的經過和她與眾不同、收視率創新高的「脫口秀」過人之處。

❶ 「**Born in 1954, Winfrey had a troubled adolescence; however, after she started living with her father, things changed.**」說明美國著名女媒體名人歐普拉的出生背景，以及早期奠定事業基礎的經過。

❷ 「**Among the outstanding achievements, the high view-rating Oprah Winfrey Show she hosted won great fame and popularity.**」敘述雖然飽受批評，她的《歐普拉脫口秀》獨樹一格，廣受好評。

❸ 「**Winfrey has attracted nationwide popularity because of her talent, passion, and persuasiveness.**」描述歐普拉的光榮得獎，以及她如何以她的才華、熱情，和她擅長說服人的特質受到全國的歡迎。

❹ 「**Oprah still humbly considers herself an ordinary person and is fully devoted to her network and charitable affairs.**」最後以敘述她的成就及致力於慈善事業、媒體事業，毫不有所鬆懈的精神作為結論。

英文講稿 便利貼光碟 2-7 Tips：虛線是重要句型！試著模仿看看，寫講稿一點都不難！

Oprah Winfrey and her Talk Show

Hi! This is Oprah Winfrey. Born in 1954, Winfrey had a troubled adolescence; however, after she stared living with her father, things changed. In college, she worked on radio and TV broadcasting. Since 1976, she has done great in talk-show hosting, acting, and managing her production company.

Among the outstanding achievements, the high view-rating Oprah Winfrey Show she hosted won great fame and popularity. She would naturally talk with guests and audiences on almost any topic, including controversial ones. She inspired enthusiasm and courage from her audience to face problems in life. Though constantly criticized, she created a public confession culture, from which her fans greatly benefited.

Winfrey has attracted nationwide popularity because of her talent, passion, and persuasiveness. Her words of wisdom and open-mindedness can always influence and encourage her audience. In 2013, she was awarded by President Obama the Presidential Medal of Freedom to honor her contributions.

The Oprah Effect made her the American media giant. Though now recognized as the richest and the most influential black person in America, <u>Winfrey still humbly considers herself an ordinary person and is fully devoted to her network and charitable affairs.</u> Isn't she incredible?

歐普拉・溫芙蕾和她的脫口秀

嗨！這是歐普拉・溫芙蕾。誕生於 1954 年，歐普拉有一段令她困擾的青少年時期；然而，自從開始和父親一起生活後，事情有所改觀了。大學時，她致力於電台和電視廣播的工作。1976 年起，她在主持脫口秀、演戲，及經營傳播公司都有出色的表現。

在眾多傑出的成就中，她所主持的高收率節目《歐普拉脫口秀》廣受好評。她會自然地和來賓及觀眾談論包括備受爭議的任何話題。她啟發觀眾的熱情及勇氣面對人生課題。雖飽受批評，她成功地塑造公開自白的文化，讓她的觀眾受益良多。

由於歐普拉的才華、熱情，和她擅長說服人的特質受到全國的歡迎。她智慧的言詞及開放的胸襟總是影響並鼓勵她的觀眾。在2013 年，歐巴馬總統頒發總統自由勳章嘉勉她的貢獻。

「歐普拉效應」使她成為美國的媒體巨擘。雖然被公認為全美最富有、最具影響力的黑人，歐普拉依舊謙虛地認為自己是個平凡人，並全力致力於廣播網和慈善事業。她是不是很了不起呢？

2-8
英文報告「臉書背後的推手：馬克・祖克伯」結合「人事物描述」句型應用

搭配文法：綜合應用句型

▶ 圖解寫作架構

Mark Zuckerberg
馬克・祖克伯

Background（背景）

The once praised "Prodigy," Zuckerberg, received fully rounded education and was brilliant in creating message programs, computer games, etc. 一度被讚揚為神童的祖克伯接受了全面教育，而且他用他聰明的頭腦發明了簡訊程式、電腦遊戲等等。

Achievements（成就）

There are over 1 billion users, which makes him the youngest and richest CEO ever. 目前有超過十億的使用者，這使得他成為有史以來最年輕、最富有的執行長。

Characteristics（特色）

With great fame and wealth, Zuckerberg remains plain, modest, and generous. 儘管有盛名及財富，祖克伯依舊保持樸實、謙虛，以及慷慨的風範。

Future Prospects（未來展望）

In 2015, with the birth of his daughter, he pledged to give 99% of his Facebook shares to help children of the following generations. 在 2015 年，隨著他女兒的誕生，他誓言要捐出臉書股份的百分之九十九來幫助未來世代的孩童。

▶ 圖解重點說分明

關於英文報告「臉書背後的推手：馬克‧祖克伯」的講稿書寫
重點：報告時各英文句型可應用於各段的引言及回顧中，讓聽眾明確
瞭解即將聽取及已聽過的內容，即可做出清晰、易懂的報告。本文介
紹「臉書」創辦人，馬克‧祖克伯的努力、成就，及貢獻。

❶ 「**The once praised "Prodigy," Zuckerberg, received fully
rounded education and was brilliant in creating message
programs, computer games, etc.**」說明美國神童祖克伯的出生
和教育背景，以及他極年輕時在電腦方面即展現的天份、創意，
及發明。

❷ 「**There are over 1 billion users, which makes him the
youngest and richest CEO ever.**」敘述多功能、廣受歡迎的社
群網站，臉書，使得祖克伯成為有史以來最年輕、最富有的執行
長。

❸ 「**With great fame and wealth, Zuckerberg remains plain,
modest, and generous.**」描述祖克伯一貫保持樸實、謙虛，慷
慨的風範。他捐贈數百萬元贊助慈善活動，並僅收取象徵性一塊
錢的年薪。

❹ 「**In 2015, with the birth of his daughter, he pledged to give
99% of his Facebook shares to help children of the
following generations.**」最後預期他將有遠見且無私地持續創
意和慈善的工作做為結論。

英文講稿 便利貼光碟 2-8 Tips：虛線是重要句型！試著模仿看看，寫講稿一點都不難！

The Person Behind Facebook: Mark Zuckerberg

Hi! This is Mark Zuckerberg. Born in 1984, he was raised in a Jewish family. Inspired by his father, he got interested in computers when little. The once praised "Prodigy," Zuckerberg, received fully rounded education and was brilliant in creating message programs, computer games, etc.

Here's the popular social networking website, Facebook, developed by Zuckerberg in 2004. With it, users can create personal profiles, make friends on line, exchange messages, and join common interest groups. There are over 1 billion users, which makes him the youngest and richest CEO ever.

With great fame and wealth, Zuckerberg remains plain, modest, and generous. He always wears the same gray T-shirt, and would donate millions for charitable causes. Besides, in 2010, he promised to donate at least 50% of his wealth to help improve the world in his lifetime. Surprisingly, as a CEO, he actually charges only one-dollar salary per year.

In 2015, with the birth of his daughter, he pledged to give

99% of his Facebook shares to help children of the following generations. Undoubtedly, Zuckerberg is a selfless person with vision worthy of our respect and admiration.

臉書背後的推手：馬克・祖克伯

嗨！這是馬克・祖克伯。誕生於 1984 年，他在猶太家庭長大。年幼時，受到父親的啟發開始對電腦感興趣。一度被讚揚為神童的祖克伯接受了全面教育，而且他用他聰明的頭腦發明了簡訊程式、電腦遊戲等等。

這就是廣受歡迎的社群網站，臉書，2004 年由祖克伯研發。藉由它，使用者可以建立個人頁面、線上交友、交換訊息，及加入相同興趣的社團。目前有超過十億的使用者，這使得他成為有史以來最年輕、最富有的執行長。

儘管有盛名及財富，祖克伯依舊保持樸實、謙虛，以及慷慨的風範。他總是穿著相同的灰色 T 恤，並捐贈數百萬元來贊助慈善活動。此外，他在 2010 年允諾今生至少要捐贈所有財產的百分之五十來幫助改善全世界。令人驚訝的是，身為執行長，他實質上每年只收取一塊錢的薪水。

在 2015 年隨著他女兒的誕生，他誓言要捐出臉書股份的百分之九十九來幫助未來世代的孩童。無疑地，祖克伯是具有遠見且無私的人，值得我們的尊敬及仰慕。

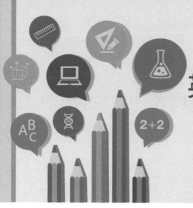

2-9
英文報告「班尼迪克・康柏拜區扮演福爾摩斯的風采」結合「人事物描述」句型應用

搭配文法：綜合應用句型

▶ **圖解寫作架構**

Benedict Cumberbatch
班尼迪克・康柏拜區

Background（背景）

Since 2010, he has successfully portrayed the intellectual detective, Sherlock Holms. 自從 2010 年以來，他成功地扮演了由十九世紀小説家，柯南・道爾撰寫的聰慧偵探，夏洛克・福爾摩斯。

Achievements（成就）

The TV series were the most watched drama series in UK and won quite a few awards. 這部電視影集在英國是收視最高的戲劇並且得到不少的獎項。

Characteristics（特色）

Besides the high quality of the adaptation, performances, and direction, it is Cumberbatch's peculiar acting skills that create a new life. 除了劇本改編、演員的演技，以及導演的高品質外，康柏拜區獨特的演技創造出新生命。

Future Prospects（未來展望）

To the thrill of all fans, Sherlock has been confirmed to return for another 5th Series. 令所有影迷非常興奮的是福爾摩斯系列被證實將會繼續開拍第五季。

圖解重點說分明

關於英文報告「班尼迪克‧康柏拜區扮演福爾摩斯的風采」的
講稿書寫

重點：報告作結論時，可藉由 in conclusion、as a result、we
conclude that⋯等歸納統整，結束報告。本文介紹扮演福爾摩斯的
英國演員：班尼迪克‧康柏拜區如何以其獨特魅力為「福爾摩斯」注
入新生命。

❶ 「**Since 2010, he has successfully portrayed the intellectual
detective, Sherlock Holms.**」說明英國演員，班尼迪克‧康柏
拜區自從 2010 年以來，成功地扮演偵探福爾摩斯。

❷ 「**The TV series were the most watched drama series in UK
and won quite a few awards.**」敘述由他扮演福爾摩斯的迷你
電視影集在英國造成轟動，不僅是收視最高的戲劇，並且獲頒不
少的獎項。

❸ 「**Besides the high quality of the adaptation, performances,
and direction, it is Cumberbatch's peculiar acting skills that
create a new life.**」描述他獨特演技及超凡魅力作出新的詮釋，
因此備受推崇。

❹ 「**To the thrill of all fans, Sherlock has been confirmed to
return for another 5th Series.**」最後以深受歡迎的福爾摩斯系
列持續開拍上映，影迷可安心愉快地觀賞福爾摩斯破解神秘犯罪
案件作為結論。

Part 1 句型篇

Part 2 圖解應用篇

英文講稿 便利貼光碟 2-9 Tips：虛線是重要句型！試著模仿看看，寫講稿一點都不難！

Benedict Cumberbatch and his Charm as Sherlock Holmes

Hi, this is Benedict Cumberbatch. Since 2010, he has successfully portrayed the intellectual detective, Sherlock Holmes, a fictitious figure created by Sir Conan Doyle.

Though an invented character, Holmes has always appealed to huge readers. When BBC invited Cumberbatch to star as Sherlock Holmes, it made a hit. The TV series were the most watched drama series in UK and won quite a few awards.

Besides the high quality of the adaptation, performances, and direction, it is Cumberbatch's peculiar acting skills that create a new life. His Holmes is cold and eccentric, with little concern for the outside world. In fact, he is observant and intellectual. Using technology to solve mysterious crimes, he turns the old Holmes into a modern dynamic superhero. He gives a new interpretation while maintaining the traditional elements and characteristics. Thus, fans worship him as the best and most fascinating Sherlock on screen.

At present, Series 4 is scheduled to release in 2017. To the thrill of all fans, Sherlock has been confirmed to return for another 5th Series. So, fans can still anticipate enjoying modern Holmes stories, with Cumberbatch solving mysteries of crimes in 221B, Baker Street, London.

班尼迪克‧康柏拜區扮演福爾摩斯的風采

嗨！這是班尼迪克‧康柏拜區。自 2010 年起，他成功地扮演柯南‧道爾杜撰的聰慧偵探，夏洛克‧福爾摩斯。

雖然是一個杜撰角色，福爾摩斯總是吸引廣大讀者。當 BBC 邀請康柏拜區主演福爾摩斯時造成轟動。這部電視影集在英國是收視最高的戲劇並且得到不少的獎項。

除了劇本改編、演員的演技，以及導演的高品質外，康柏拜區獨特的演技創造出新生命。他所扮演的福爾摩斯性格冷漠古怪，疏離於外在世界。事實上，他富觀察力且機智過人。他使用科技來解決神秘的犯罪案件，並將舊式的福爾摩斯轉成為現代朝氣蓬勃的超級英雄。他賦予新的詮釋，同時又保存了傳統的元素和特質。因此，影迷推崇他為螢幕上最佳且最迷人的福爾摩斯。

目前，第四季預計在 2017 年上映。令所有影迷非常興奮的是福爾摩斯系列被證實將會繼續開拍第五季。因此，影迷仍可以期待觀賞現代福爾摩斯的故事，由康柏拜區在倫敦貝克街的 221B 寓所來破解神秘的犯罪案件。

2-10

英文報告結合人事物描述
句型應用小練習

▶ 英文報告、人事物描述句型小回顧

　　「人事物描述」英文報告時，在開場白引言、中間串場，及結束回顧作結論方面皆可利用各種句型讓聽眾注意報告的人物及相關主題。譬如利用對等及附屬連接詞句型的運用可使人物報告精簡扼要，內容有物。利用轉承副詞的句型可引領出前後連貫、行文流暢的報告。亦可藉由用於結論的句型歸納統整結論，結束報告。英文報告過程中宜靈活運用各類句型，依場合情境，增添變化。再者，措辭應簡易口語，活潑生動，藉以吸引在場聽眾全程的注意，進而做出令人印象深刻、成功過人的報告。

▶ 文法句型補一補

( ) 1. The teacher announced _____ due to the coming typhoon, the field trip was cancelled.

(A) that   (B) which   (C) this   (D) what

( ) 2. _____ air and water, human beings could not survive.

(A) With   (B) If   (C) Without   (D) If not

( ) 3. Ann can speak several languages, _____ her brother is good at science.

(A) after   (B) while   (C) because   (D) until

( ) 4. _____ fooling around, or you may end up a loser.

(A) Stops   (B) To stop   (C) Stop   (D) Stopped

( ) 5. Tired _____ Tim was, he went on staying up all night.

(A) as   (B) after   (C) but   (D) since

( ) 6. Pandas are rare animals. _____, it's our duty to protect them from being extinct.

(A) However   (B) Besides   (C) Firstly   (D) Therefore

Part 1 句型篇

Part 2 圖解應用篇

201

▶ 答案與解析

1. (A) that

題目中譯 老師宣佈由於颱風即將來臨，戶外教學被取消了。

答案解析 句型 S + announce that + S + V ... 中，及物動詞 announce 後面必須搭配由 that 引導的名詞子句做為受詞。故應選 (A) that。

2. (C) Without

題目中譯 沒有空氣和水，人類無法生存。

答案解析 由後半段可得知是假設語氣的用法，前半段 air and water 是兩個名詞，前面應搭配介系詞。故應選 (C) Without。

3. (B) while

題目中譯 安會説數種語言，而她的哥哥擅長於科學。

答案解析 兩個前後語意相反成對比的子句要用附屬連接詞 while 連接。故應選 (B) while。

4. (C) Stop

題目中譯 不要再到處鬼混了，否則你終將一事無成。

答案解析 祈使句中，主詞 You 省略，後面必須搭配原形動詞。故選 (C) Stop。

5. (A) as

題目中譯 提姆雖然很累，他仍然整夜持續地熬夜。

答案解析 根據固定句型，「Adj + as/though + S + V ...，S + V ... 雖然……」，答案應選 (A) as。

6. (D) Therefore

題目中譯 貓熊是稀有動物，因此保護它們免於滅絕是我們的責任。

答案解析 說明理由的轉承副詞要用 therefore。故應選 (D) Therefore。

▶ 寫作老師巧巧說

　　撰寫「人事物描述」英文報告時，除了在開場白、中間串場，及結束作結論方面可利用到各種活用的句型外，在描述的人物及相關主題上，引言部份，可由描述主角人物的「背景」做一開始，本文部份，則由主角人物的「成就」及「特色」兩部份做為主要的介紹描述內容，最後，可以「未來展望」結論段做為全文的結束。如此即可造就完整連貫的描述，讓讀者對介紹人物及相關主題有具體全面的瞭解。

3-1
英文作文「養寵物的經驗」結合「故事與情緒描述」句型應用

搭配文法：現在分詞與過去分詞句型

▶ **圖解寫作架構**

Paragraph 1（第一段）

Topic Sentence（主題句）

I will never forget the happy moments I used to share with my pet dog, Rover. 我將永遠難忘過去和我的寵物狗，羅佛，共享的快樂時光。

Supporting Sentence（支持句）

Rover was never too busy a friend to make me feel lonely. 羅佛從來就不會是因為太忙碌而使我感到寂寞的朋友。

Concluding Sentence（結尾句）

I was so delighted to have such a great companion. 我很高興擁有如此絕佳的同伴。

▶ **圖解重點說分明**

關於「養寵物的經驗」英文作文的書寫

重點：「故事、情緒描述」英文作文 2 個段落可由各段的「Topic Sentence（主題句）」、「Supporting Sentence（支持句）」，以及「Concluding Sentence（結尾句）」三大方面寫出完整達意的段落文章。

第一段（Paragraph 1）：

❶「**I will never forget the happy moments I used to share with my pet dog, Rover.**」為中心思想。說明作者懷念和 Rover 過去的快樂相處。

❷「**Rover was never too busy a friend to make me feel lonely.**」為文章主體，透過「支持句」敘述 Rover 對作者無止盡的忠誠及重視。

❸「**I was so delighted to have such a great companion.**」為本段的結論，描述作者慶幸有此一忠實好友，為此段作一總結。

第二段（Paragraph 2）：

❶「**The tragic loss of Rover came as a shock when we were happy to have him.**」本段的「主題句」。說明作者驟失愛犬的失落及震驚。

❷「**We felt guilty and depressed about his missing, especially me, heart-broken for losing the genuine friend.**」「支持句」進一步敘述作者的懊悔及難過，用以達成全段文章「統一性」（Unity）的特色。

❸「**How I wish one day he would appear in front of me and we could have happy times together again!**」為本段的結論，描述作者期盼 Rover 能回返，重拾往昔歡樂時光，為此段及全文作一總結。

英文作文 便利貼光碟 3-1 Tips：套色和虛線處都是重要句型！可試著仿照該文風格，寫出你自己的一篇文章！

提示：請以 "A Pet-Keeping Experience" 為主題，寫一篇 120 至 150 個字的英文作文，說明養寵物的經驗及感想。

A Pet-Keeping Experience

I will never forget the happy moments I used to share with my pet dog, Rover. Rover was a cute, playful golden retriever with thick yellow hair all over. He was a true friend and companion to me. When I came back home from school, he would passionately come running to me, jump onto my arm, and lick my face. We would often play in the park, joyfully chasing and running around. Rover was never too busy a friend to make me feel lonely. He would always willingly keep me company and faithfully protect me from danger. I was so delighted to have such a great companion.

The tragic loss of Rover came as a shock when we were happy to have him. One afternoon, Rover ran away from home when the front door was carelessly wide open, and never returned. Probably his playful mind carried him too far away, thus causing his getting lost. Feeling terribly sad, we looked for him and posted his pictures everywhere; however, there was no sign of his. We felt guilty and depressed about his missing, especially me, heart-broken for losing the genuine friend. Till today, I miss him every day and truly regret about the carelessness. How I wish one day he would appear in front of me and we could have happy times together again!

養寵物的經驗

我將永遠難忘過去和我的寵物狗，羅佛，共享的快樂時光。羅佛是一隻全身佈滿厚重黃毛、可愛頑皮的黃金獵犬。對我來說，他是一個真正的朋友以及同伴。當我從學校返家時，他會熱情地跑向我，跳上我的手臂，並且舔我的臉。我們常常在公園裡玩，開心地到處追逐奔跑。羅佛從來就不會是因為太忙碌而使我感到寂寞的朋友。他總是樂意地陪伴我，並且忠心地保護我免於危險。我很高興能擁有如此絕佳的同伴。

正當我們慶幸有羅佛的時候，他突如其來的失蹤令我們感到震驚哀傷。某天下午，當大門意外地敞開時，羅佛奪門而出，一去不返。也許他的玩心把他帶離得太遠，因此導致他的失蹤。帶著極度悲傷懊惱的心情，我們到處尋找並張貼他的照片，但是一無所獲。我們對於他的失蹤，內心感到罪惡及沮喪，尤其是我，為失去一名真正的朋友心碎。直到今日，我每天懷念他並深深地後悔當時的粗心大意。我多期盼有一天他會出現在我的面前，我們將可以再次共享快樂的時光！

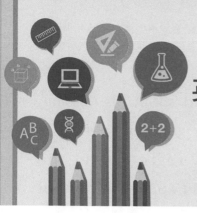

3-2
英文作文「面對同儕壓力」結合「故事與情緒描述」句型應用

搭配文法：關係子句

▶ **圖解寫作架構**

Paragraph 1（第一段）

Topic Sentence（主題句）

Peer pressure bothered me a lot last Friday afternoon.
上禮拜五下午，同儕壓力帶給我很大的困擾。

Supporting Sentence（支持句）

Caught in a dilemma, I tactfully declined by replying I had night classes to attend. 深陷於進退兩難的困境中，我巧妙地以晚上有課為由來婉拒。

Concluding Sentence（結尾句）

I'm glad I made the decision because they failed in the attempt and got their lesson. 我很高興我做了那個決定，因為他們的計畫失敗並且獲得了教訓。

▶ **圖解重點說分明**

關於「面對同儕壓力」英文作文的書寫

重點：英文作文兩個段落可由各段以單刀直入的主題句切入主題，並由確實舉例、分析闡明的支持句來發展段落，最後則以歸納結論作為結束而寫出完整達意的段落文章，文章前後呼應，條理分明。

第一段（Paragraph 1）：

❶「**Peer pressure bothered me a lot last Friday afternoon.**」
主題句直接點出同儕壓力帶來的壓力，十分困擾作者。

❷「**Caught in a dilemma, I tactfully declined by replying I had night classes to attend.**」支持句敘述巧妙脫身進退兩難困境之道。

❸「**I'm glad I made the decision because they failed in the attempt and got their lesson.**」本段的結論，描述作者慶幸做出正確抉擇。

第二段（Paragraph 2）：

❶「**However, when asked to do something inappropriate, we should follow certain rules not to risk academic career.**」是第二段的主題句。說明作者認為有些原則應予以堅守，以成功地處理同儕壓力。

❷「**So, leave them and make new friends that are more like us, though this may seem a sad thing to do.**」支持句敘述更多應堅守的原則。

❸「**By doing the above, the impact of peer pressure will surely be reduced and we can live a much happier life.**」本段的結論，唯有減少同儕壓力的衝擊力量，我們才有可能過更快樂的生活。

英文作文 便利貼光碟 3-2 Tips：套色和虛線處都是重要句型！可試著仿照該文風格，寫出你自己的一篇文章！

提示：以 "Dealing With Peer Pressure" 為主題，寫一篇 120 至 150 個字的英文作文，說明你曾有過同儕壓力的經驗及處理壓力的方法。

Dealing with Peer Pressure

Peer pressure bothered me a lot last Friday afternoon. Tom and Luke, bright but playful, were my two good friends. Last Friday after school, they planned to shoplift a high-priced PS4. Needing a third person to watch out for them, they asked me to join. Caught in a dilemma, I tactfully declined by replying I had night classes to attend. At that instant, I could sense their anger and dissatisfaction with me. However, I think making the right decision is one key point to cope with peer pressure. I'm glad I made the decision because they failed in the attempt and got their lesson.

It's true that teenagers are eager to be identified by peers. However, when asked to do something inappropriate, we should follow certain rules not to risk academic career. To begin with, we should distinguish between right and wrong and firmly say "No!" Secondly, not offending peers, we can make excuses to leave or change the topic. Thirdly, genuine friends won't pressure us to do false things. So, leave them and make new friends that are more like us, though this may seem a sad thing to do. Finally, with more wisdom and experiences, our parents and teachers are trustworthy and communicative to offer us practical advice. By doing the above, the impact of peer pressure will surely be reduced and we can live a much happier life.

面對同儕壓力

　　上禮拜五下午，同儕壓力帶給我很大的困擾。聰明但是調皮的湯姆和路克是我兩個要好的朋友。上禮拜五放學後，他們計畫到店裡去偷竊昂貴的 PS4 電玩。他們需要第三個人來把風，於是請求我加入。深陷於進退兩難的困境中，我巧妙地以晚上有課為由來婉拒。在那瞬間，我可以感受到他們對我的憤怒以及不滿。然而，我認為做出正確的決定是對抗同儕壓力關鍵的做法。我很高興我做了那個決定，因為最後他們的計畫失敗並且獲得了教訓。

　　青少年固然十分渴望被同儕所認同。然而，當被請求去做不合宜的事情時，我們仍應當遵循特定的規則，以免危及到自己的學業。首先，我們應該明辨是非，並且堅定地說 "不"。第二點，不要去得罪同儕，我們可以製造藉口離去，或是改變話題。第三點，真正的好友不會逼迫我們做錯誤的事情。所以，不妨離開他們去結交和我們相似的新朋友，雖然這麼做似乎有點悲哀。最後，有著豐富智慧和經歷的師長們一向是值得信賴並易於溝通，可提供我們實際的忠告。藉由實施上列的方法，同儕壓力的衝擊力量必將大大地減少，我們便可以過更快樂的生活。

3-3

英文作文「『精靈寶可夢』，好玩或不好玩？」結合「故事與情緒描述」句型應用

搭配文法：分詞構句句型

▶ 圖解寫作架構

Paragraph 1（第一段）

Topic Sentence（主題句）

Recently, I love to play the smartphone game, *Pokémon GO*, and have mixed feelings. 最近我喜愛玩手機遊戲，"精靈寶可夢"，這個遊戲讓我產生了錯綜複雜的感覺。

Supporting Sentence（支持句）

Also, the playing of the game is easy, and with so many different kinds of monsters, I never get tired or bored. 再者，玩這個遊戲很容易上手，而且有著各式各樣的精靈可以捕捉，我從來都不覺得累或者無聊。

Concluding Sentence（結尾句）

All in all, undoubtedly, it's great fun to play *Pokémon* outdoors. 總之，無疑地，到戶外玩精靈寶可夢非常好玩。

▶ 圖解重點說分明

關於「『精靈寶可夢』，好玩或不好玩？」英文作文的書寫重點：作文題目使用問句引發讀者的興趣與深思是成功的開頭方法。其後由「主題句」引領出具張力的正反兩面論點時，巧妙地使用有層

Chapter 3 英文作文結合故事與情緒描述句型應用

3-3 ｜英文作文「『精靈寶可夢』，好玩或不好玩？」結合「故事與情緒描述」句型應用 — 搭配文法：分詞構句句型

次感的「轉承語」，如 first、besides、in addition、finally、all in all 等，使得兩段的「支持」文字達到有組織，頗具說服力的功效。

第一段（Paragraph 1）：

❶「**Recently, I love to play the smartphone game, *Pokémon GO*, and have mixed feelings.**」主題句說明作者對 *Pokémon* 錯綜複雜的感覺。

❷「**Also, the playing of the game is easy, and with so many different kinds of monsters, I never get tired or bored.**」為文章主體，逐句透過「支持句」敘述 *Pokémon* 的好處及作者喜愛它的原因。

❸「**All in all, undoubtedly, it's great fun to play *Pokémon* outdoors.**」為本段的結論，描述作者肯定 *Pokémon* 的優點，為此段作一總結。

第二段（Paragraph 2）：

❶「**However, I get influenced by the potential danger caused by it.**」是第二段的主題句。說明作者親身體會到 *Pokémon* 帶來的負面效應。

❷「**My staring at the screen closely while walking makes me frequently bump into other pedestrians.**」進一步敘述作者感受到的缺點。

❸「**With all the confusion and conflicts, is it really fun to play *Pokémon*?**」為本段結論，以對 *Pokémon* 的質疑，作為全文的總結。

英文作文 便利貼光碟 3-3 Tips：套色和虛線處都是重要句型！可試著仿照該文風格，寫出你自己的一篇文章！

提示：請以 "Pokémon, Fun or No Fun?" 為主題，寫一篇 120 至 150 個字的英文作文，描述一項你喜愛的休閒活動及從中得到的心得。

Pokémon, Fun or No Fun?

Recently, I love to play the smartphone game, *Pokémon GO*, and have mixed feelings. I think it is great fun to play *Pokémon GO* for its several advantages. First, unlike the usual smartphone games, playing *Pokémon* forces the players who seldom move around to go outdoors. In addition, while playing it, I get acquainted with players from different regions with same interests. Also, the playing of the game is easy, and with so many different kinds of monsters, I never get tired or bored. What is even better is that the catching of the monsters amuses me a lot, which also costs me nothing. All in all, undoubtedly, it's great fun to play *Pokémon* outdoors.

However, I get influenced by the potential danger caused by it. First, to quickly catch monsters, I have to always look at the screen, which greatly endangers my eyesight. Also, I am so concentrated on it that I neglect my studies. And my parents,

Chapter 3 英文作文結合故事與情緒描述句型應用

3-3 ｜ 英文作文「『精靈寶可夢』，好玩或不好玩？」結合「故事與情緒描述」句型應用 — 搭配文法：分詞構句句型

who put a high premium on my schoolwork, get angry and scold me furiously. Besides, my staring at the screen closely while walking makes me frequently bump into other pedestrians. In addition, on the street, to catch *Pokémon* monsters, drivers park their cars at will and get red tickets, which results in their angry quarrels with the policemen. With all the confusion and conflicts, is it really fun to play *Pokémon*?

「精靈寶可夢」，好玩或不好玩？

　　最近我喜愛玩手機遊戲，「精靈寶可夢」，這個遊戲讓我產生了錯綜複雜的感覺。我認為寶可夢很好玩因為它具有幾項優點。首先，不同於一般的手機遊戲，玩寶可夢迫使原先很少到處走動的玩家們開始走向戶外。此外，玩精靈遊戲時，我認識了許多來自不同地方以及擁有共同興趣的玩家。再者，玩這個遊戲很容易上手，而且有著各式各樣的精靈可以捕捉，我從來都不覺得累或者無聊。更棒的是，除了捕捉精靈很開心之外，我不需要花任何一毛錢。總之，無疑地，到戶外玩精靈寶可夢非常好玩。

　　然而，玩寶可夢使我被遊戲過程中潛藏的危機所影響。首先，為了要儘快抓到精靈，我必須時時盯著手機螢幕看，嚴重地危及到我的視力。再者，我太過專注於玩寶可夢，以至於疏忽了課業。這使得一向重視課業的父母生氣了，並憤怒地責罵我。此外，我邊走路邊緊盯著手機螢幕使我常常撞到其他的行人。另外，在街道上為了要捕捉精靈，駕駛隨意停車而被開罰單，導致他們和警察發生嚴重的爭執。看著這一切的混亂和衝突，精靈寶可夢真的好玩嗎？

3-4
英文作文「一次難忘的旅遊」結合「故事與情緒描述」句型應用

搭配文法：比較級與最高級句型

▶ **圖解寫作架構**

Paragraph 1（第一段）

Topic Sentence（主題句）

The graduation trip in my second year in senior high was the most unforgettable trip to me. 我高二的畢業旅行對我來說是最難忘的一次旅遊。

Supporting Sentence（支持句）

We were as happy as skylarks. 我們如同雲雀一般地快樂自在。

Concluding Sentence（結尾句）

However, some noises from far away aroused our curiosity. 然而，遠方傳來的噪音引起了我們的好奇。

▶ **圖解重點說分明**

關於「一次難忘的旅遊」英文作文的書寫

重點：「一次難忘的旅遊」描述重點在「難忘」的焦點上。藉由「對照」（Contrast）的寫作技巧，作者對於「歡樂」旅遊的難忘，對比於親眼目睹溺水事件而對「悲傷」旅遊的難忘，突顯文章的張力。

全文的對比清晰有力，結論有理，頗能搏得讀者認同。

第一段（Paragraph 1）：

❶ 「**The graduation trip in my second year in senior high was the most unforgettable trip to me.**」說明作者畢業之旅是難忘的一次旅遊。

❷ 「**We were as happy as skylarks.**」「支持句」敘述畢業旅遊的開心。

❸ 「**However, some noises from far away aroused our curiosity.**」本段的結論，但同時技巧地轉折至另一場景，即引人悲傷的溺水事件。

第二段（Paragraph 2）：

❶ 「**Something bad seemed to have happened!**」是第二段的主題句。說明作者由高興轉而難過的感受天壤之別，印象深刻難忘。

❷ 「**The sad and intense atmosphere then made us feel like crying too.**」是本段的「支持句」，敘述作者深受哀傷氣氛影響，也十分難過。

❸ 「**I think I will never forget the trip and will be careful in everything I do so as not to have regrettable consequences.**」為本段的結論，作者警惕自己要小心行事，安全為重，為此段及全文作一總結。

英文作文 便利貼光碟 3-4 Tips：套色和虛線處都是重要句型！可試著仿照該文風格，寫出你自己的一篇文章！

提示：請以 "An Unforgettable Trip" 為主題，寫一篇 120 至 150 個字的英文作文，描述一次難忘的旅遊經驗，並說明難忘的原因。

An Unforgettable Trip

The graduation trip in my second year in senior high was the most unforgettable trip to me. We went to Kenting then and had a great time all the way. We chatted, laughed, and sang a lot of songs. The louder we sang, the happier we became. We were as happy as skylarks. When we were at the beach, we enjoyed the beautiful scenery and went swimming happily. Besides, we barbecued on the sand and enjoyed the easy and pleasant atmosphere. In the evening, we sat on the beach looking at the beautiful sunset and had the most wonderful time ever. However, some noises from far away aroused our curiosity.

Something bad seemed to have happened! Crowded people around a certain spot surprised us, and we ran there as fast as we could. A drowning boy was dragged from the water, but after immediate rescue, he still died. Beside the little boy, his parents cried and shouted tragically, yelling his name. The sad and intense atmosphere then made us feel like crying too. To the poor parents, losing their dearest son was the cruelest punishment that they had ever gone through. To our sorrow, the happy trip should become so terrible and tragic. I think I will never forget the trip and will be careful in everything I do so as not to have regrettable consequences.

一次難忘的旅遊

　　我高二的畢業旅行對我來説是最難忘的一次旅遊。我們當時到墾丁，並且一路玩得很開心。我們閒聊、大笑，還有唱很多首歌。我們唱得越大聲就越覺得開心，我們如同雲雀一般地快樂自在。當我們在沙灘上時，我們欣賞美麗的風景，快樂地游泳。此外，我們在沙地上烤肉，享受輕鬆愉快的氣氛。在傍晚時，我們坐在沙灘上眺望美麗的夕陽，度過最美妙的時光。然而，遠方傳來的噪音引起了我們的好奇。

　　似乎有不好的事發生了！有一大群人團團圍在一個定點，令人驚訝之餘，我們儘快地跑去觀看。一個溺水的男孩從水中被拉出來，經過立即的搶救仍不幸身亡。男孩的雙親在一旁悲傷地哭喊他的名字。當時悲傷緊張的氣氛，也讓我們悲從中來。對這對可憐的父母來説，失去他們最親愛的兒子是這一生所經歷過最殘酷的懲罰。令我們難過的是，快樂的出遊竟然變成如此地恐怖悲傷。我想我將永遠難忘這趟旅程，並且會小心謹慎行事，為的是不希望有憾事發生。

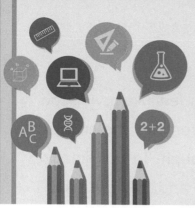

3-5
英文作文「幫助他人」結合「故事與情緒描述」句型應用

搭配文法：倒裝句句型

▶ **圖解寫作架構**

Paragraph 1（第一段）

Topic Sentence（主題句）

A seemingly small and random act of kindness may make a big difference. 一個似乎微小而不經意的善行可能造成很大的不同。

Supporting Sentence（支持句）

Kasey's kind act made the old lady's days bright again. 凱西的善行使得這名老婦人的人生再度明亮起來。

Concluding Sentence（結尾句）

Obviously, his little kindness greatly changed the old lady's world. 很明顯地，他小小的善意大大地改變了這名老婦人的世界。

▶ **圖解重點說分明**

關於「幫助他人」英文作文的書寫

重點：藉由一則新聞報導的內容，闡述「幫助他人」所發揮營造雙贏的益處，條理分明，言之成理，激勵讀者助人益己，尋求快樂之源。主題句、支持句，以及結尾句書寫得宜，再加上轉承語順暢連結，完

整達意的段落文章，成功地發揮出主題重點。

第一段（Paragraph 1）：

❶「**A seemingly small and random act of kindness may make a big difference.**」此「主題句」點出不經意的助人舉動可帶給他人快樂。

❷「**Kasey's kind act made the old lady's days bright again.**」為文章主體，透過「支持句」舉例敘述助人可發揮極大的影響力。

❸「**Obviously, his little kindness greatly changed the old lady's world.**」敘述凱西助人改變他人的世界並且因此意外獲得大筆小費的回報。

第二段（Paragraph 2）：

❶「**Helping others creates a win-win situation.**」是第二段的主題句。說明助人可得雙贏的好處。

❷「**In fact, doing others a little favor can make both the recipients and the givers happy.**」「支持句」闡述助人者及接受幫助者同樣受益。

❸「**Thus, let's start helping others generously so as to create a world full of concern, warmth and happiness.**」為本段的結論，呼籲大家共同發揮助人精神，締造溫馨歡樂的世界，為此段及全文作一總結。

英文作文 便利貼光碟 3-5 Tips：套色和虛線處都是重要句型！
可試著仿照該文風格，寫出你自己的一篇文章！

提示：請以 "Helping Others" 為主題，寫一篇 120 至 150 個字的
英文作文，敘述一件助人為樂的事件，並說明助人帶來的好處。

Helping Others

A seemingly small and random act of kindness may make a big difference. Kasey Simmons, a waiter, was tipped $500 by a grateful daughter. Only from the napkin she scribbled did Kasey realize he lifted the spirits of her mother. On the anniversary of her husband's death, the old lady was at a loss in the checkout line in a market. Hardly did anybody help but passed her by. Kasey paid the bill and warmly praised her beauty. Kasey's kind act made the old lady's day bright again, and so happy was she that she smiled a lot. Obviously, his little kindness greatly changed the old lady 's world.

Helping others creates a win-win situation. It's sad that due to the fast pace of life, most people are indifferent. In fact, doing others a little favor can make both the recipients and the givers happy. Not only can we improve their lives but we are spiritually repaid with joy by the good deeds we do. Were there many people like Kasey, we would be always inspired and delighted. Thus, let's start helping others generously so as to create a world full of concern, warmth and happiness.

幫助他人

　　一個似乎微小而不經意的善行可能造成很大的不同。服務生凱西・西蒙斯，曾得到一名心存感激的女兒所給美金 500 元的小費。凱西從她潦草寫的餐巾紙了解他無意間提振她母親的心情。老婦人在丈夫去世周年當天，在市場的結帳隊伍中茫然困惑。幾乎無人給予協助，只是從她身邊走過。凱西為她付帳單並溫馨讚美她的美麗。凱西的善行使得這名老婦人的人生再度明亮起來，而她快樂到一直開心微笑。很明顯地，他小小的善意大大地改變了這名老婦人的世界。

　　幫助他人可創造雙贏的局面。說來悲傷，由於今日生活步調的快速，人們大多冷漠。事實上，幫別人一點小忙，可以使得接受者與付出者雙方快樂。藉由我們的善行，不僅可以改善他人的生活，我們也在精神上得到回報。假使天底下有許多像凱西這樣的人，我們將總是精神振奮且快樂。因此，讓我們開始慷慨地幫助他人，如此一來便可以創造關切、溫馨，並且快樂的世界。

3-6
英文作文「誰找到歸誰嗎？」結合「故事與情緒描述」句型應用

搭配文法：對等與平行結構句型

▶ 圖解寫作架構

Paragraph 1（第一段）

Topic Sentence（主題句）

I don't think finders should be keepers. 我不認為誰找到就該歸誰。

Supporting Sentence（支持句）

You may end up both in prison and in miserable loneliness. 你最後的結局可能是被關到監獄裡，並且身處於悲慘的寂寞情境中。

Concluding Sentence（結尾句）

Thus, to keep a clear conscience rather than a criminal record, I think honesty is the best policy. 因此，為了要保持清白的良知而非犯罪的紀錄，我認為誠實為上策。

▶ 圖解重點說分明

關於「誰找到歸誰嗎？」英文作文的書寫

重點：「論說文」的寫法可以一段論說內容，一段舉實例來證實論點。第一段先明確、堅定地論述原則，第二段舉出強而有力的例子使文章具有說服力。本文先說理，再藉由一則新聞報導的內容，敘述因

Chapter 3 英文作文結合故事與情緒描述句型應用

3-6 ｜英文作文「誰找到歸誰嗎？」結合「故事與情緒描述」句型應用 – 搭配文法：對等與平行結構句型

不誠實而得到的報應，藉以警惕大眾「誠實為上策」的真諦。

第一段（Paragraph 1）：

❶「**I don't think finders should be keepers.**」主題句先表明作者的論點。

❷「**You may end up both in prison and in miserable loneliness.**」為文章主體，透過「支持句」敘述不誠實可能面對的懲罰及報應。

❸「**Thus, to keep a clear conscience rather than a criminal record, I think honesty is the best policy.**」為本段的結論，描述作者堅信欺騙的行為不僅導致坐牢，也會良心不安，為此段作總結。

第二段（Paragraph 2）：

❶「**The recent news about a dishonest girl can be a good example to illustrate my idea.**」是第二段的主題句。作者舉例證實論點。

❷「**She preferred to enjoy her luck rather than stick to honesty.**」本句是「支持句」，敘述文中主角一時貪念，鑄成大錯的悲慘情境。

❸「**From her example, I firmly believe that finders should never be keepers.**」為本段的結論，作者重申「誠實為上策」的重要。

英文作文 便利貼光碟 3-6 Tips：套色和虛線處都是重要句型！
可試著仿照該文風格，寫出你自己的一篇文章！

提示：以 "Are Finders Keepers?" 為主題，寫 120 至 150 個字的英文作文，闡述 "Finders Keepers" 的觀念，並舉一實例說明你的論點。

Are Finders Keepers?

I don't think finders should be keepers. On the one hand, what belongs to others doesn't belong to you. You should return what you find, or it's actually stealing and deception. If you are dishonest, others will doubt your integrity and truthfulness. They will not respect but despise you. You may end up both in prison and in miserable loneliness. On the other hand, your wrong doing is in fact not only against the law but against your moral conscience and ethical codes. The feeling of guilt will torture you all the time, though nobody may know anything about it. Thus, to keep a clear conscience rather than a criminal record, I think honesty is the best policy.

The recent news about a dishonest girl can be a good example to illustrate my idea. In Australia, a Malaysian girl, Christine Lee, accidentally became a millionaire by finding $ 4.6 million in her deposit account. So happy was she that she did

Chapter 3 英文作文結合故事與情緒描述句型應用

3-6 ｜英文作文「誰找到歸誰嗎？」結合「故事與情緒描述」句型應用 – 搭配文法：對等與平行結構句型

not inform the bank of their errors but pursued luxurious joyfulness by living in a mansion, buying fancy handbags, etc. She preferred to enjoy her luck rather than stick to honesty. To her sadness, what she did was exposed and she got arrested. The greedy girl not only had to return the money but was charged with theft, ending up in prison. From her example, I firmly believe that finders should never be keepers.

誰找到歸誰嗎？

我不認為誰找到就該歸誰。一方面來說，屬於別人的並不屬於你。你應該歸還你所找到的，否則它事實上是偷竊和欺騙的行為。假使你不誠實，別人會懷疑你的廉潔以及真誠。他們不會尊敬你，反而會鄙視你。你最後的結局可能是被關到監獄裡，並且身處於悲慘的寂寞情境中。另一方面來說，你錯誤的行為，事實上不僅違法，而且違反你的道德良知以及倫理規範。雖然別人可能不知道，但是罪惡感會一直折磨你。因此，為了要保持清白的良知而非犯罪的紀錄，我認為誠實為上策。

最近有關於一名不誠實女孩的報導可以充分地說明我的看法。在澳洲，有一名叫克莉絲汀‧李的馬來西亞籍女孩，無意間發現存款帳戶中被存入 460 萬美金而成為百萬富翁。她是如此地快樂以至於並未告知銀行他們的錯誤，反而是藉由住豪宅、買炫麗的手提包等，追求奢華的享受。她寧可享受她的好運氣，而不願堅守誠實的原則。令她很悲傷的是，她的罪行最後曝光，遭到警方逮捕。這名貪心的女孩，不僅須歸還這筆錢，並且被以竊盜罪起訴，最後結局是啷噹入獄。以她為例，我堅信誰找到絕對不該歸誰。

3-7
英文作文「我最喜愛的節日」結合「故事與情緒描述」句型應用
搭配文法：綜合應用句型

▶ 圖解寫作架構

Paragraph 1（第一段）

Topic Sentence（主題句）

Among all the festivals, I like the Western holiday, Christmas, the best. 在所有的節慶當中，我最喜歡西方的節日，聖誕節。

Supporting Sentence（支持句）

I enjoy the warm and happy atmosphere everywhere. 我喜歡四處散發溫馨歡樂的氣氛。

Concluding Sentence（結尾句）

As a whole, Christmas is a joyous time for reunion and appreciation. 整體而言，聖誕節是團聚和感恩的歡樂時節。

▶ 圖解重點說分明

關於「我最喜愛的節日」英文作文的書寫

重點：第一段描述聖誕節各項吸引人的特色，並以發揮耶誕精神作為結尾。第二段則引用世界文學名著，《耶誕頌歌》感動人心的故事闡述耶誕節的內涵，發人深省，敘述清晰，前後文章呼應統一。

第一段（Paragraph 1）：

❶「**Among all the festivals, I like the Western holiday, Christmas, the best.**」主題句具體說明作者最喜歡的節日是聖誕節。

❷「**I enjoy the warm and happy atmosphere everywhere.**」透過「支持句」敘述作者對聖誕節有特殊感受及聖誕節豐富的意象和意義。

❸「**As a whole, Christmas is a joyous time for reunion and appreciation.**」結論句總結聖誕節團圓及感恩的意義。

第二段（Paragraph 2）：

❶「**One thing about Christmas that impresses me most is *Christmas Carol*, a classic novel written by Charles Dickens.**」說明《耶誕頌歌》是作者對聖誕節相關印象深刻的古典小說並敘述本書的背景。

❷「**Only after his own witnesses of being despised and deserted does he repent.**」敘述吝嗇富人史庫奇歷經奇遇而體會耶誕真諦的情境。

❸「**I'm truly touched by the meaningful story, and I think it's important that we bear Christmas spirit in mind while enjoying the Christmas time.**」本段的結論，心靈深受感動的作者期盼讀者發揮耶誕精神。

Part 1 句型篇

Part 2 圖解應用篇

英文作文 便利貼光碟 3-7 Tips：虛線處是重要句型！可試著仿照該文風格，寫出你自己的一篇文章！

提示：請以 "My Favorite Festival" 為主題，寫一篇 120 至 150 個字的英文作文描述你最喜愛的節日及此節日一項令你印象深刻的事物。

My Favorite Festival

Among all the festivals, I like the Western holiday, Christmas, the best. Firstly, during Christmas time, colorful and twinkling Christmas trees with beautiful ornaments are seen in the stores and the streets, accompanied by Santa Claus giving little gifts to passers-by. I enjoy the warm and happy atmosphere everywhere. In addition, family and friends exchange presents and greeting cards to pass along blessings and good will. It's a magnificent time to give love and blessing through mutual concern. Finally, we merrily get together to appreciate peace and luck that bless us through the whole year. As a whole, Christmas is a joyous time for reunion and appreciation.

One thing about Christmas that impresses me most is *Christmas Carol*, a classic novel written by Charles Dickens. Ebenezeer Scrooge, an old miser, changes his ideas about Christmas after the visit of three ghosts. They relentlessly show him his miserable past, present stubborn attitudes, and pathetic future yet to come. Only after his own witnesses of being despised and deserted does he repent. He awakens, joyfully finding that it's only a nightmare, and he makes redemption by spreading out Christmas spirit to the full. I'm truly touched by the meaningful story, and I think it's important that we bear Christmas spirit in mind while enjoying the Christmas time.

我最喜愛的節日

在所有的節慶當中，我最喜歡西方的節日，聖誕節。首先，在聖誕時節，商店裡和街道上可見到裝飾有美麗飾品、五彩繽紛，而且閃閃發亮的耶誕樹，伴隨著聖誕老公公發送禮物給行人。我喜歡四處散發溫馨歡樂的氣氛。此外，家人和朋友互相交換禮物和賀卡來傳送祝福以及善意。這是經由彼此關心傳送愛及祝福的絕佳時刻。最後，我們歡樂地聚集在一起感謝一整年庇佑我們的和平和幸運。整體而言，聖誕節是團聚和感恩的歡樂時節。

有關於聖誕節令我印象最深刻的一件事物是由查爾斯·狄更斯所寫的經典小說，《耶誕頌歌》。一個年邁的吝嗇鬼，艾比尼·史庫奇，在三個鬼的拜訪之後改變他對聖誕節的看法。他們無情地帶他看到了他悲慘的過去、現在偏執的態度，以及可悲的未來。唯有在他親眼目睹自己被鄙視、遺棄之後，他才悔悟。他醒過來後，開心地發現原來一切只是一場惡夢，他藉由全心全意地散播聖誕精神來彌補過去的錯誤。我確實十分感動於這個富含意義的故事，並且認為在享受聖誕佳節時，我們謹記聖誕節的精神及意義是很重要的。

3-8
英文作文「網際網路」結合 「故事與情緒描述」句型應用

搭配文法：綜合應用句型

 圖解寫作架構

Paragraph 1（第一段）

Topic Sentence（主題句）

In my opinion, the Internet has brought us a lot of benefits. 依我之見，網際網路為我們帶來許多好處。

Supporting Sentence（支持句）

What's more, through the Internet, a lot of things can be easily achieved. 更進一步而言，透過網際網路，我們可以輕易地完成許多事。

Concluding Sentence（結尾句）

The Internet is really amazing and helpful! 網際網路真的是既神奇又助益良多！

▶ 圖解重點說分明

關於「網際網路」英文作文的書寫

重點：論說文的文字必須明確有力，論點則須合理中肯，足以說服讀者。本文由各段的主題句、支持句，以及結尾句逐點分析「網際網路」的優缺點，段落文章有確切地達到完整及說服的功效。

第一段（Paragraph 1）：

❶「**In my opinion, the Internet has brought us a lot of benefits.**」為此段的主旨。說明「網際網路」的多項優點。

❷「**What's more, through the Internet, a lot of things can be easily achieved.**」為文章主體，支持強調「網際網路」的全方位功能。

❸「**The Internet is really amazing and helpful!**」為本段的結論，作者讚嘆「網際網路」無遠弗屆，為此段作一總結。

第二段（Paragraph 2）：

❶「**In spite of all the advantages the Internet has, it has given rise to many potential problems.**」本段主題句，說明「網際網路」的缺點。

❷「**Still another drawback of the Net is that we may easily fall victim to vicious frauds or unpredictable threats.**」此支持句進一步敘述「網際網路」是一個虛擬世界，它的各種缺點陷阱足以為人們帶來禍害。

❸「**Accordingly, with the far-reaching and convenient Internet, we had better be careful not to get addicted and should make the most of it.**」為本段的結論，描述作者期盼讀者留意「網際網路」的缺點，並善用它的優點，謹慎行事，為此段及全文作總結。

英文作文 便利貼光碟 3-8 Tips：虛線處是重要句型！可試著仿照該文風格，寫出你自己的一篇文章！

提示：請以 "The Internet" 為主題，寫一篇 120 至 150 個字的英文作文說明你對網際網路的看法。

The Internet

In my opinion, the Internet has brought us a lot of benefits. It gives us conveniences and access to information. To begin with, we can instantly know the major world news by browsing websites of international news. In addition, we can gather all kinds of information via the search engines with only a click of the mouse. What's more, through the Internet, a lot of things can be easily achieved. For example, we can watch interesting films, play on-line games, and make purchases through e-commerce. Also, by making international e-pals, we can get to know foreign cultural values and broaden our horizons. The Internet is really amazing and helpful!

In spite of all the advantages the Internet has, it has given rise to many potential problems. One disadvantage is that all the information on the Net isn't necessarily correct and cannot be fully depended. Another problem it causes is that people tend to get so addicted to it that they may end up losing concentration, wasting time, or even committing crimes. Still another drawback of the Net is that we may easily fall victim to vicious frauds or unpredictable threats. After all, the world it creates for us is a virtual one. Accordingly, with the far-reaching and convenient Internet, we had better be careful not to get addicted and should make the most of it.

網際網路

　　依我之見，網際網路為我們帶來許多好處。它提供我們便利以及資訊的取得。首先，我們藉由瀏覽國際新聞網站可以立即得知重大的事件。此外，我們只要點一下滑鼠透過搜尋引擎就可以收集各種資訊。更進一步而言，透過網際網路，我們可以輕易地完成許多事。舉例來說，我們可以觀看有趣的影片、玩線上遊戲，並且可以透過電子商務購買物品。再者，藉由結交國際網友，我們可以瞭解外國的文化價值，拓展我們的視野。網際網路真的是既神奇又助益良多！

　　儘管網際網路有如此多的優點，但是它也製造許多潛在的問題。一個缺點是在網際網路上所有的資訊並非全然的正確，不能夠全面仰賴。另外一個它導致的問題是，人們傾向於過度沉迷於網路以致於演變的結果是注意力不集中、浪費時間，甚至從事網路犯罪。網際網路還有另一項缺失是我們很輕易地成為惡意的詐欺或是無法預測的威脅的受害者。畢竟，網際網路為我們所創造的是一個虛擬的世界。因此，雖擁有無遠弗屆、相當便利的網際網路，我們最好要小心不要沉迷上癮，並且應該發揮它最大的功用。

3-9
英文作文「全球暖化」結合「故事與情緒描述」句型應用

搭配文法：綜合應用句型

▶ 圖解寫作架構

Paragraph 1（第一段）

Topic Sentence（主題句）

Nowadays, global warming is the most serious environmental problem that poses threats to the earth. 今日而言，全球暖化是對地球造成威脅最嚴重的環境問題。

Supporting Sentence（支持句）

Owing to the rise of temperature, a lot of serious disasters have arisen. 由於氣溫上升，許多嚴重的災難因而發生。

Concluding Sentence（結尾句）

A lack of environmental awareness contributes to its growing increasingly serious. 環保意識的缺乏導致全球暖化日益嚴重。

▶ 圖解重點說分明

關於「全球暖化」英文作文的書寫

重點：敘述「全球暖化」的兩個段落均由各段的主題句有具體的開頭，另有支持句的支持與發展，再有結尾句做統整及結論，組織續

密。轉承語的使用自然通順，故能產生段落連貫、行文統一的文章。

第一段（Paragraph 1）：

❶「**Nowadays, global warming is the most serious environmental problem that poses threats to the earth.**」為文章整體的中心思想。說明「全球暖化」是當今最具威脅性的環境污染問題。

❷「**Owing to the rise of temperature, a lot of serious disasters have arisen.**」為文章主體，透過「支持句」敘述「全球暖化」產生的各種問題。

❸「**A lack of environmental awareness contributes to its growing increasingly serious.**」為本段的結論，描述人類缺乏環保意識才導致「全球暖化」的惡化，為此段作一總結。

第二段（Paragraph 2）：

❶「**Fortunately, humans are now finding ways to cope with the problem.**」是第二段的主題句。說明幸好人們開始重視此議題。

❷「**There are several things we can do to lessen the impact.**」本段的「支持句」，提出具體的改善方法，以減緩「全球暖化」的劣境。

❸「**So, let's work together to ensure a better tomorrow!**」為本段的結論，描述作者期盼藉由大眾的努力，創造優質地球，為全文作總結。

英文作文 便利貼光碟 3-9 Tips：虛線處是重要句型！可試著仿照該文風格，寫出你自己的一篇文章！

提示：請以 "Global Warming" 為主題，寫一篇 120 至 150 個字的英文作文，說明全球暖化造成的影響及人類因應的對策。

Global Warming

Nowadays, global warming is the most serious environmental problem that poses threats to the earth. The earth is getting warmer because of too much heat-trapping carbon dioxide in the atmosphere. Owing to the rise of temperature, a lot of serious disasters have arisen, such as the melting of the polar ice, the raising of the sea levels, the crisis of food shortage, the extinction of endangered species, and so on. And the causes may include industrial overdevelopment, deforestation, greenhouse gases from too much emission of fossil fuels, and the more. In fact, sadly to say, it is human beings that cause the tragic crises to happen. A lack of environmental awareness contributes to its growing increasingly serious.

Fortunately, humans are now finding ways to cope with the problem. There are several things we can do to lessen the impact. First, we should boost energy conservation. Use electricity economically and always take the mass transportation. Second, it also helps a lot to recycle more and buy less. Third, alternative energy resources such as solar or wind power should be developed. Fourth, stop destroying the ecosystems by deforestation. And last, it is imperative for scientists to develop low-carbon technology for a major breakthrough. All in all, as members of the global village, we should spare no efforts to protect the environment not only for ourselves but for future generations.

全球暖化

今日而言，全球暖化是對地球造成威脅最嚴重的環境問題。地球變得越來越溫暖是由於大氣層中充滿過多形成熱氣的二氧化碳。由於氣溫上升，許多嚴重的災難因而發生，譬如極地冰塊的融化、海平面上升、食物短缺的危機、物種瀕臨滅絕等等。導致的原因可能包含工業過度發展、森林砍伐、化石燃料釋放過多的溫室氣體等等。事實上，很不幸的一點是，是人類本身導致悲慘危機的發生。環保意識的缺乏導致全球暖化日益嚴重。

幸好，人們現在正在尋找對抗全球暖化的方法。我們可以做一些事來減緩衝擊的力量。首先，我們應該提倡節約能源。節制用電，並且多多搭乘大眾交通工具。第二點，多回收，少購物，也可以有很大的幫助。第三點，多發展如太陽能或風力發電的替代能源。第四點，停止砍伐森林而破壞生態系統。最後，科學家們的當務之急是以發展出低碳科技來做出重大突破。總之，身為地球村的成員，不僅為我們自己，更為未來的下一代，我們應該不遺餘力地保護環境。

3-10

英文作文結合故事與情緒描述
句型應用小練習

▶ 英文報告、人事物描述句型小回顧

　　撰寫「故事、情緒描述人事物描述」英文作文時，可依三個部分：主題句（**Topic Sentence**）、段落發展（**Paragraph Development**）、及結論句（**Concluding Sentence**）書寫。主題句說明整段文章的主旨，應力求精簡具體。段落發展用以支持主題句，可利用解釋或舉例的方式，提出支持主題句的論點。結論句總結段落，用不同的文字重述主題句，或將內容做個評論總結，重申文章主旨。文章中宜靈活運用各類句型，增添變化。如此便能寫出切題又兼具充實內容的佳作。

▶ **文法句型補一補**

( ) 1. With his eyes _____, Simon enjoyed the classical music on his old couch.

(A) close   (B) closed   (C) closing   (D) to close

( ) 2. Under no circumstance _____ make the same mistake again!

(A) have you   (B) you should

(C) you have   (D) should you

( ) 3. The earlier you get started, the _____ you'll get to the MRT station.

(A) soon   (B) soonest   (C) sooner   (D) less soon

( ) 4. Tom and Nick were _____ by the teacher because of their misbehavior in class.

(A) punish   (B) punishing   (C) punishes   (D) punished

( ) 5. Jeff is handsome and humorous, and that's the reason _____ he is popular with girls.

(A) why   (B) which   (C) who   (D) while

( ) 6. Emily was kind-hearted, so she preferred to tell a white lie _____ tell the truth.

(A) rather not   (B) would

(C) rather than   (D) than

答案與解析

1. (B) closed

題目中譯 賽門閉著眼睛坐在他老舊的沙發上享受古典音樂。

答案解析 根據「獨立分詞構句」句型：With + N + pp～，S + V～，
應選 close 的過去分詞，表示被動，即 (B) closed。

2. (D) should you

題目中譯 你絕對不可以再犯相同的錯誤！

答案解析 Under no circumstances + aux + S + VR～，or + S + V～
是倒裝句的固定句型。故應選 (D) should you。

3. (C) sooner

題目中譯 你越早出發，你就可以越早到達捷運站。

答案解析 The＋比較級…，the＋比較級…，是表示「比例」比較的
固定句型。故應選 (C) sooner。

4. (D) punished

題目中譯 湯姆和尼克由於在課堂上行為不良被老師處罰。

答案解析 過去分詞和 be 動詞連用，形成被動語態。故選 (D)
punished。

5. (A) why

題目中譯 傑夫既英俊又幽默，而這就是他受女孩歡迎的原因。

答案解析 關係子句用法中，The reason 後要搭配疑問詞 why，後接
子句，以說明理由。故應選 (A) why。

6. (C) rather than

題目中譯 愛蜜莉心地善良，所以她寧可説善意的謊言而不願意説出真相。

答案解析 連接詞片語 prefer to ... rather than ... 意指「寧願……，而不願……」，用來説明平行對等的情境，是固定的片語。故應選 (C) rather than。

▶ 寫作老師巧巧説

　　撰寫「故事、情緒描述人事物描述」英文作文時，要符合寫作原則，即段落文章應要能達「連貫」（Coherence）與「統一」（Unity）的原則。要達到「連貫」（Coherence）的原則，句子與句子間可多利用「轉承語」（Transitional Words）來連接文章間各個論點、描述。要達到「統一」（Unity）的原則，即要避免寫出與主題不相干的句子（Irrelevant Sentences）或具有同樣語意的冗贅句子（Redundant Sentences），可搭配各種不同段落寫作的技巧，以達到統一、有條不紊的效用。如描寫文中先寫一般情境，再描述特殊性。敘事文可依時間先後順序或空間遠近書寫。論説文及説明文則可依重要性的順序，由最不重要延伸到最重要等。掌握上述兩項原則即可以使全文不至雜亂離題，而能保持流暢連貫、統整並且有組織。

4-1
英文信件「求職信」結合「英文書信用語」句型應用
搭配文法：原因與讓步句型

▶ **圖解寫作架構**

稱呼語（Salutation）

Dear Mr. Sullivan:

引文與目的（Introduction and Purpose）

The reason why I write is that I am interested in your ad of a position for a salesperson. 我寫這封信的原因是我對於您在廣告上刊載徵求業務員的職缺感興趣。

內文 1（Paragraph 1）

I recently completed my military service and I am looking for a job opportunity as a salesperson. 我最近剛退伍，目前正在尋找業務員的工作機會。

內文 2（Paragraph 2）

Because of my enthusiasm and willingness, I am sure to specialize as a salesperson. 由於我的熱忱和意願，我必將專精於擔任業務員。

結論與期許（Conclusion and Wishes）

I look forward to hearing from you for the opportunity of an interview. 我期盼能夠接到您的來信，提供面試的機會。

結尾辭與簽名（Closing and Signature）

Truly yours,
Mike Yang

▶ 圖解重點說分明

關於「求職信」的書寫

重點：撰寫求職信應要簡明扼要，重視合宜誠懇的語氣及態度，敘述要完整並具說服力。大致說明自己的學歷、技能，及經驗。談論背景概述和具體成就之外，更要強調本身潛力及學習的意願，主動積極，藉以加深主管的印象，順利博取面試的機會。

1 「**The reason why I write is that I am interested in your ad of a position for a salesperson.**」說明引發作者撰寫求職信，應徵業務員的動機原由及目的。

2 「**I recently completed my military service and I am looking for a job opportunity as a salesperson.**」此部份強調應徵者不僅學有專長，認真、有效率地擔任助理所得的打工經驗亦訓練有成，表現出色。

3 「**Because of my enthusiasm and willingness, I am sure to specialize as a salesperson.**」應徵者具優異的人格特質、英語語言、人際溝通，及電腦方面的技能等。雖然工作經驗不多，但有能力且頗具學習意願，應能勝任工作。

4 「**I look forward to hearing from you for the opportunity of an interview.**」最後以誠摯的態度，期盼獲得面試的機會作為結論。

英文信件 便利貼光碟 4-1 Tips：套色部分是可替換的地方！虛線是重要句型！

An Application Letter

Dear Mr. Sullivan:

With this letter, I would like to introduce myself. The reason why I write is that I am interested in your ad of a position for a salesperson.

As my attached resume shows, I am a college graduate with a major in International Trade. I recently completed my military service and I am looking for a job opportunity as a salesperson. My work experience includes part-time work as an administrative assistant in my department in junior and senior years. Though it was only a part-time job, I worked diligently and efficiently, and I did well at my assistant work.

I am independent, communicative, and trustworthy. Despite the fact that I don't have too much work experience, I am keen and fast to learn. I am proficient in English, and good at oral communication and computer skills. Because of my enthusiasm and willingness, I am sure to specialize as a salesperson. Now, I hope to seek the possibility of becoming your staff. I can assure you that I will do my utmost to make valuable contributions.

I look forward to hearing from you for the opportunity of an interview. Thank you for your time and consideration.

Truly Yours,
Mike Yang

求職信

敬愛的蘇利文先生：

　　藉由這封信，我想作自我介紹。我寫這封信的原因是我對於您在廣告上刊載徵求業務員的職缺感興趣。

　　正如我附上的履歷表所顯示，我是主修國際貿易的大學畢業生。我最近剛退伍，目前正在尋找業務員的工作機會。我的工作經驗包含大三大四時在我的系上打工擔任行政助理。雖然它只是一個打工工作，但是我很勤奮而且有效率，在助理工作上表現得很傑出。

　　我很獨立、善於溝通，並且值得信賴。儘管我沒有太多的工作經驗，但是我很積極而且學得很快。我有純熟的英語能力，擅長於口語表達以及電腦技能。由於我的熱忱和意願，我必將專精於擔任業務員。此時，我希望尋求成為貴公司職員的可能性。我可以向您保證我會盡我最大的努力為貴公司帶來有價值的貢獻。

　　我期盼能夠接到您的來信，提供面試的機會。感謝您撥冗費心。

您真誠的楊麥克

4-2
英文信件「詢問信」結合「英文書信用語」句型應用

搭配文法：目的與結果句型

▶ 圖解寫作架構

稱呼語（Salutation）

Dear Mr. Cooper:

引文與目的（Introduction and Purpose）

I am writing this letter to inquire about the products of your company. 我寫這封信來詢問貴公司的產品。

內文 1（Paragraph 1）

I would very much like to learn more about your products. 我非常想多了解有關於貴公司產品的一切。

內文 2（Paragraph 2）

Consequently, we hope to get the newest catalogue, detailed prices, payment terms, and samples of the goods from you. 於是，我們希望從貴公司獲得最新的產品目錄、商品價格、付款條件，以及商品樣本。

結論與期許（Conclusion and Wishes）

Please send the above-mentioned items and information as soon as possible, so that we can make our decisions early. 請儘快寄出上述的項目及資訊，如此一來我們便可提早做出決定。

結尾辭與簽名（Closing and Signature）

Yours very truly,
Jerry Wang

▶ 圖解重點說分明

關於「詢問信」的書寫

重點：撰寫詢問信要明確地敘述詢問的內容，一個段落談論一個重點。第一段先說明目的，第二、三段即告知寫詢問信的原由及詢問想知道的訊息，第四段即作結論，期望對方如何配合，感謝合作等。全文語氣宜誠懇直接，簡潔完整，便可達到書寫本詢問信的目的。

❶「I am writing this letter to inquire about the products of your company.」說明作者撰寫此詢問信的目的是詢問對方公司產品。

❷「I would very much like to learn more about your products.」此部份強調作者公司想瞭解對方產品相關資訊，而有意訂購合作。

❸「Consequently, we hope to get the newest catalogue, detailed prices, payment terms, and samples of the goods from you.」在此段作者希望對方提供目錄、價格表、樣本等以供參考，衡量是否訂購商品。

❹「Please send the above-mentioned items and information as soon as possible, so that we can make our decisions early.」最後以誠摯的態度，期盼早日取得查詢的資訊，方可儘早做出決定，作為全文的結論。

英文信件 便利貼光碟 4-2 Tips：套色部分是可替換的地方！虛線是重要句型！

An Inquiry Letter

Dear Mr. Cooper:

I am Jerry Wang, the manager of Mason Company. I am writing this letter to inquire about the products of your company.

Last month, in the Trade Fair, I had an interesting talk with Mr. Williams. He recommended your esteemed company as one of the most reliable manufacturers. As a result, I have the opportunity to contact you. I would very much like to learn more about your products. We will have a steady demand if they're at moderate prices.

This year we aim to raise the quality of our products, so we are eager to find suppliers for refined merchandise. Consequently, we hope to get the newest catalogue, detailed prices, payment terms, and samples of the goods from you. Also, in order to make long-term business partnership, we need to know if you offer extended warranty.

Please send the above-mentioned items and information

Chapter 4 英文信件結合英文書信用語句型應用
4-2 ｜英文信件「詢問信」結合「英文書信用語」句型應用 – 搭配文法：目的與結果句型

Part

1

句型篇

Part

2

圖解應用篇

as soon as possible, so that we can make our decisions early. Your time and effort will be highly appreciated.

Yours very truly,
Jerry Wang

詢問信

敬愛的庫柏先生：

　　我是王傑利，梅森公司的經理。我寫這封信來詢問貴公司的產品。

　　上個月在商業展覽會中，我和威廉斯先生有過有趣的談話。他推薦貴公司是最可靠的製造廠商之一。因此，我有這個機會來跟您聯絡。我非常想多了解有關於貴公司產品的一切。假使價格合宜，我們將固定購買貴公司的產品。

　　今年我們公司的目標是提升產品的品質，所以我們熱切地尋找優質商品的供應廠商。於是，我們希望從貴公司獲得最新的產品目錄、商品價格、付款條件，以及商品樣本。此外，為了要建立長期的合作關係，我們需要了解貴公司是否有提供商品的延長保固。

　　請儘快寄出上述的項目及資訊，如此一來我們便可提早做出決定。我們將非常感謝您所付出的時間和努力。

　　　　　　　　　　　　　　　　　　　您最真誠的王傑利

4-3
英文信件「請求信」結合
「英文書信用語」句型應用
搭配文法：時間與條件句型

▶ **圖解寫作架構**

稱呼語（Salutation）
Dear Mr. Baker:

引文與目的（Introduction and Purpose）
If possible, we request to act as an exclusive agency for the promotion of your products. 假使可能，我們請求擔任促銷貴工廠產品的獨家代理商。

內文 1（Paragraph 1）
We are experienced and well-trained in opening up new markets for our clients. 我們在為客戶開發新市場上非常有經驗並且訓練有素。

內文 2（Paragraph 2）
As long as you decide to entrust us with the exclusive agency, we can start acting for you. 一旦您決定要把獨家代理權託付給我們，我們便可以開始為你們代理。

結論與期許（Conclusion and Wishes）
Provided that you should be interested in our potentiality, please do not hesitate to contact us. 假使您對我們的潛力有興趣，請不要遲疑，馬上與我們聯絡。

結尾辭與簽名（Closing and Signature）
Very truly yours,
David Wu

圖解重點說分明

關於「請求信」的書寫

重點：撰寫請求信應要簡短明確，請求內容的敘述要直接完整。語法上則應多用主動語態，避免過於深奧的用字或複雜的文法，可讓收信人快速瞭解寄信人的需求或請求內容，進而快速地作回應。

❶「**If possible, we request to act as an exclusive agency for the promotion of your products.**」寄信人撰寫此信請求擔任代理商。

❷「**We are experienced and well-trained in opening up new markets for our clients.**」此部份強調請求獨家代理權的寄信人公司不僅經驗豐富，並且也訓練有素，必可為客戶開拓市場。

❸「**As long as you decide to entrust us with the exclusive agency, we can start acting for you.**」只要一經准許擁有獨家代理權，寄信人公司馬上可為客戶進行代理工作。

❹「**Provided that you should be interested in our potentiality, please do not hesitate to contact us.**」最後以誠摯的態度，期盼獲得代理權機會作為結論。

英文信件 便利貼光碟 4-3 Tips：套色部分是可替換的地方！虛線是重要句型！

A Request Letter

Dear Mr. Baker:

This March, in Shanghai Spring Fair, we were deeply impressed by the newest products exhibited by your factory. If possible, we request to act as an exclusive agency for the promotion of your products.

Until now, our company has established excellent reputation as an active agency in this area. We are experienced and well-trained in opening up new markets for our clients. In addition, we have close contact and fine relationship with regional wholesalers. After careful survey, our company has confidence in developing a profitable selling line for your goods. We can create substantial orders and bring about a big increase in your sales.

Our specialization can offer you guarantee of granting our request. As long as you decide to entrust us with the exclusive agency, we can start acting for you. For further discussion, before May 1, please enclose us with your relevant terms and detailed conditions. We believe, if the terms meet with our approval, we'll achieve mutual benefits by close collaboration.

<u>Provided that you should be interested in our potentiality,</u> <u>please do not hesitate to contact us.</u> We await your affirmative reply.

Very truly yours,
David Wu

請求信

敬愛的貝克先生：

今年三月，在上海春季展覽會中，我們對貴工廠展示的最新產品印象十分深刻。假使可能，我們請求擔任促銷貴工廠產品的獨家代理商。

迄今，我們公司在本區已建立卓越獨家代理公司的聲譽。我們在為客戶開發新市場上非常有經驗並且訓練有素。此外，我們與地區批發商有密切的接觸以及良好的關係。經過仔細評估，我們公司有信心可以為您的商品開發利潤豐厚的銷售線。我們可以為貴工廠創造大量的訂單，並大大增加你們產品的銷售量。

我們的專業可以提供貴工廠批准我們請求的保證。一旦您決定要把獨家代理權託付給我們，我們便可以開始為你們代理。為了進一步的討論，請於五月一日前附上相關條件和細節事項。我們相信，假使條件在我們批准的範圍內，我們可以藉由密切合作達成共同利益。

假使您對我們的潛力有興趣，請不要遲疑，馬上與我們聯絡。我們等待您肯定的答覆。

您最真誠的吳大衛

4-4
英文信件「抱怨信」結合
「英文書信用語」句型應用
搭配文法：強調與焦點句型

▶ **圖解寫作架構**

稱呼語（Salutation）
Dear Mr. Jones:

引文與目的（Introduction and Purpose）
I regret to say that we have complaints to make concerning the products we purchased from you. 我很遺憾地要告訴您，我們要對向您購買的產品提出抱怨。

內文 1（Paragraph 1）
No sooner had we received the goods from our 27th July order than we found your factory made two serious mistakes in the shipment. 我們一收到七月二十七日的貨品馬上就發現貴公司在運送過程中犯下兩個嚴重的錯誤。

內文 2（Paragraph 2）
Little do we doubt of your taking prompt remedial measures. 我們確信貴公司將會快速地採取補救措施。

結論與期許（Conclusion and Wishes）
We will continue our working relationship only with your explanation and response. 唯有在您提出說明和做出回應後，我們才將繼續我們的合作關係。

結尾辭與簽名（Closing and Signature）
Yours very truly,
Alan Chang

圖解重點說分明

關於「抱怨信」的書寫

重點：撰寫抱怨信要切中要點，語氣宜堅定友善，具體地陳述事實經過及想傳達的訊息，使用具建設性的態度及建言，可加深負責主管的印象及瞭解，便能順利且快述取得問題妥善處理解決的機會。

❶「**I regret to say that we have complaints to make concerning the products we purchased from you.**」以友善堅定的語氣説明引發寄信者撰寫抱怨信的原由及目的。

❷「**No sooner had we received the goods from our 27th July order than we found your factory made two serious mistakes in the shipment.**」此部份具體陳述抱怨的內容，供對方快速瞭解出差錯的地方。

❸「**Little do we doubt of your taking prompt remedial measures.**」抱怨信撰寫者在此段中使用具建設性的態度及建言，加深負責人的印象及瞭解，使問題可以順利快述地妥善處理。

❹「**We will continue our working relationship only with your explanation and response.**」最後以誠摯的態度，期盼對方快速處理，方能延續友好商業夥伴的關係作為結論。

Part 1 句型篇

Part 2 圖解應用篇

英文信件 便利貼光碟 4-4 Tips：套色部分是可替換的地方！虛線是重要句型！

A Complaint Letter

Dear Mr. Jones:

It is our long-established business relationship that we have always valued. Nevertheless, I regret to say that we have complaints to make concerning the products we purchased from you.

No sooner had we received the goods from our 27th July order than we found your factory made two serious mistakes in the shipment. In the first place, what went wrong with the merchandise was that Case 18 and 19 did not contain the goods we ordered. The other was that three cases of your shipments arrived in either a slightly or a badly damaged condition.

Were you not going to do the following to fix the problems right away, we might ask for a refund. Firstly, we demand that you ship the two cases of correct goods we ordered as soon as possible. Secondly, send a capable sales representative to examine and take care of the damaged merchandise. Enclosed are the original order and the lists of the faulty and damaged goods. Little do we doubt of your taking prompt remedial measures.

Your immediate attention on this matter is strongly urged. We will continue our working relationship only with your explanation and response.

Yours very truly,
Alan Chang

抱怨信

敬愛的瓊斯先生：

　　我們長久建立的合作關係一向是我們所重視的。但是，我很遺憾地告訴您，我們要對向您購買的產品提出抱怨。

　　我們一收到七月二十七日的貨品就馬上發現貴公司在運送過程中犯下兩個嚴重的錯誤。首先，這批商品出問題的狀況是第十八號及十九號箱內的貨物並不是我們所訂購的。另一項問題是有三箱運送的貨物在抵達時有稍微受損或嚴重受損的情況。

　　如果貴公司不立即採取下列行動以修正問題，我們很可能會要求退款。第一點，我們要求您儘快運送我們原先訂購的兩箱正確的商品。第二點，請派送一名能幹的業務代表來檢閱並處理受損的商品。附件的內容是原始的訂購單以及錯誤和受損貨品的表單。我們確信貴公司將會快速地採取補救措施。

　　我們強烈要求您儘速處理此事。唯有在您提出說明和做出回應後，我們才將繼續我們的合作關係。

　　　　　　　　　　　　　　　　　　　您最真誠的張艾倫

4-5
英文信件「回覆信」結合 「英文書信用語」句型應用

搭配文法：比較與對比句型

▶ 圖解寫作架構

稱呼語（Salutation）

Dear Mr. Peterson:

引文與目的（Introduction and Purpose）

I need to make some explanation and express my apology. 我必須做說明並表達我的歉意。

內文 1（Paragraph 1）

As opposed to your usual reaction to our yearly increase in prices, you sent us a letter complaining about their being too high. 相對照於往常您對於我們每一年價格提升的反應，您來信抱怨價格太高了。

內文 2（Paragraph 2）

I can assure you that we will offer not only goods more refined than before but more satisfactory after-sales service. 我可以向您保證，我們不僅將提供比以往更優質的商品，也提供更滿意的售後服務。

結論與期許（Conclusion and Wishes）

Your understanding is highly appreciated. 非常感謝您的諒解。

結尾辭與簽名（Closing and Signature）

Faithfully yours,
Tom Lin

▶ **圖解重點說分明**

關於「回覆信」的書寫

重點：撰寫回覆信要針對對方的需求或怨言予以回覆，真心誠意，據實以告，清楚地敘述回覆的細節或預定採取的補救措施，取信對方。語氣及態度應誠懇確實，敘述完整具說服力，並提出具體作法。

❶ 「**I need to make some explanation and express my apology.**」敘述引發作者撰寫回覆信的目的是對於產品漲價提出道歉及說明理由。

❷ 「**As opposed to your usual reaction to our yearly increase in prices, you sent us a letter complaining about their being too high.**」此部份強調作者重視對方不滿的抱怨，藉此信做出道歉的回應與解說。

❸ 「**I can assure you that we will offer not only goods more refined than before but more satisfactory after-sales service.**」作者提出保證，貨品價格雖提高，品質更佳之外，售後服務的效率亦隨之提升。

❹ 「**Your understanding is highly appreciated.**」最後以誠摯的態度，期盼獲得對方的信任及體諒作為結論。

Part **1** 句型篇

Part **2** 圖解應用篇

英文範文

英文信件 便利貼光碟 4-5 Tips：套色部分是可替換的地方！虛線是重要句型！

A Response Letter

Dear Mr. Peterson:

I am writing this letter in reply to your letter of 16th February. I need to make some explanation and express my apology.

In the notification we made last week, we announced the price increase from 1 February on and enclosed the new price lists of this year's newest products. Compared with the old prices, the new products are one and a half times as expensive as before. As opposed to your usual reaction to our yearly increase in prices, you sent us a letter complaining about their being too high. However, there're reasons and absolute guarantee from us.

Each year, we spare no efforts to raise the quality standard of our products. In contrast with the old products, our new products are of much higher quality. Thus, we are paying a lot more for the raw materials. In addition, due to another contributing factor, the inflation, we cannot but raise the prices. Nevertheless, I can assure you that we will offer not only goods more refined than before but more satisfactory after-sales service.

I trust this has clarified your doubts and once again I apologize for the inconveniences caused. Your understanding is highly appreciated.

Faithfully yours,
Tom Lin

回覆信

敬愛的彼得森先生：

　　我寫這封信來回覆您二月十六日的來信，我必須做説明並表達我的歉意。

　　上週我們所做的通知中，我們宣布從二月一日起提高價格並附上今年最新產品的新價格表。和舊的價格比較起來，今年新的價格是以往的一倍半貴。相對照於往常您對於我們每一年價格提升的反應，您來信抱怨價格太高了。但是，這麼做是有理由的，而且您可以得到我們絕對的保證。

　　每一年我們都不遺餘力地提升我們產品品質的標準。相反於過去的產品，我們的新產品具備有更高的品質。因此，我們為原物料付出較多的價錢。此外，由於另一個導致漲價的原因，通貨膨脹，我們不得不提升價格。然而，我可以向您保證，我們不僅將提供比以往更優質的商品，也將提供更令人滿意的售後服務。

　　我相信這封信能夠澄清您的疑問，並且我再度為帶來的不便向您道歉。非常感謝您的諒解。

您忠實的林湯姆

4-6
英文信件「感謝信」結合「英文書信用語」句型應用

搭配文法：特殊動詞句型

▶ 圖解寫作架構

稱呼語（Salutation）

Dear Mr. Williams:

引文與目的（Introduction and Purpose）

With this letter, I would express my sincere thankfulness. 藉由這封信，我想表達我誠摯的謝意。

內文 1（Paragraph 1）

We regard it as an honor that you show great confidence in us and place orders without hesitation. 我們把您對我們展現極大的信心而且毫不遲疑地下訂單視為一項榮耀。

內文 2（Paragraph 2）

To show our gratitude, we would like to invite you to our Year-End Dinner Party on January 10. 為了表示我們的感激，我們想邀請您來參加我們一月十日的尾牙餐宴。

結論與期許（Conclusion and Wishes）

We appreciate your solid support and look forward to seeing you present. 我們感謝您穩固的支持，並且誠摯期盼您的光臨。

結尾辭與簽名（Closing and Signature）

Yours very faithfully,
John Tang

🔻 圖解重點說分明

關於「感謝信」的書寫

重點：撰寫感謝信時，語氣（Tone）應要熱忱殷勤，可細數對方優點。文字確切簡明，充份表達感謝之情，表明重視對方。主動邀約參加尾牙餐宴，不僅可表達謝意，亦可進一步持續未來業務的發展。

❶「**With this letter, I would express my sincere thankfulness.**」說明感謝信的目的在於感謝對方多年來的支持。

❷「**We regard it as an honor that you show great confidence in us and place orders without hesitation.**」此部份強調感恩於對方極度的信任及慷慨持續的訂單。

❸「**To show our gratitude, we would like to invite you to our Year-End Dinner Party on January 10.**」作者邀請對方參加年末感恩餐宴，藉此表達誠摯的謝意及來年繼續合作的意願。

❹「**We appreciate your solid support and look forward to seeing you present.**」最後盛情邀約，並期盼對方能出席餐宴作為結論。

英文信件 便利貼光碟 4-6 Tips：套色部分是可替換的地方！虛線是重要句型！

An Appreciation Letter

Dear Mr. Williams:

I am replying to your ordering letter of 2nd December. With this letter, I would express my sincere thankfulness. For the past ten years, you have maintained fine relationship with us, which we cannot thank enough.

We regard it as an honor that you show great confidence in us and place orders without hesitation. It is our policy to try hard and spend much time perfecting our goods. The efforts and painstaking seldom stop us from going on and we are lucky to have your encouragement. Also, through your recommendation, the new clients you introduced would often willingly establish business relationship with us. We truly appreciate your support!

To show our gratitude, we would like to invite you to our Year-End Dinner Party on January 10. In the year to come, we hope to extend further cooperation with you. If you aren't satisfied with us, please do not hesitate to inform us of what we should improve. Your comments and suggestions will arouse our enthusiasm to make progress and prosper.

Enclosed is the invitation card, and you're heartily welcome to join us. <u>We appreciate your solid support and look forward to seeing you present.</u>

Yours very faithfully,
John Tang

感謝信

敬愛的威廉斯先生：

　　我要對您十二月二日的訂購信做回覆。藉由這封信，我想表達我誠摯的謝意。過去十年來，貴公司持續地與我們保持良好的關係，這是我們非常感謝的。

　　我們把您對我們展現極大的信心而且毫不遲疑地下訂單視為一項榮耀。我們努力並且花很多時間使我們的商品完美是我們公司一向的政策。這份努力和辛勤很少阻擋我們持續向前，而我們很幸運地擁有您的鼓勵。此外，經由您的推薦，您所介紹的新客戶時常很樂意地與我們建立商業關係。我們真的很感謝您的支持！

　　為了表示我們的感激，我們想邀請您來參加我們一月十日的尾牙餐宴。在來年，我們期盼能與您發展更進一步的合作關係。假使您對我們的服務不滿意，請不要遲疑於告知我們該改進的地方。您的評論及建議將會激發我們的熱忱去追求進步及蓬勃的發展。

　　附上邀請函，我們竭誠歡迎您的參與。我們感謝您穩固的支持，並且誠摯期盼您的光臨。

您最忠實的唐約翰

4-7

英文信件「恭賀信」結合「英文書信用語」句型應用

搭配文法：綜合應用句型

▶ **圖解寫作架構**

稱呼語（Salutation）

Dear Philip,

引文與目的（Introduction and Purpose）

Congratulations on your dream come true!

內文 1（Paragraph 1）

Your spirit and persistence in fulfilling your dream is admirable and we all share the joy and honor with you. 你實現夢想的精神及恆心值得讚佩，我們與你共同分享喜悅和榮耀。

內文 2（Paragraph 2）

I think it's great that you plan to join your dream student club, get to know more friends, and make an around-the-island trip. 我覺得你計畫加入夢想中的社團、多認識朋友，及環島旅行是很棒的。

結論與期許（Conclusion and Wishes）

With our hearty congratulations on your splendid success, we truly hope that you'll enjoy your college life and make the best of it! 真誠地致上我們對你傑出成就的恭賀，我們真心期盼你將享受並善用你的大學生活！

結尾辭與簽名（Closing and Signature）

Always affectionately, Uncle Franck

圖解重點說分明

關於「恭賀信」的書寫

重點：撰寫恭賀信時，應要熱絡真誠，不僅嘉許對方的辛勤付出，並讚揚對方的成就。親切誠懇的語氣，足以表達親朋之間的喜悅慶賀。具體地給予未來計畫的提醒建議及祝福，更顯關心溫馨。

❶「**Congratulations on your dream come true!**」說明引發作者撰寫恭賀信的目的是恭喜對方進入理想的大學，並勉勵提醒應有的態度。

❷「**Your spirit and persistence in fulfilling your dream is admirable and we all share the joy and honor with you.**」此部份讚許對方追求夢想付出的精神可嘉，親朋與有榮焉。

❸「**I think it's great that you plan to join your dream student club, get to know more friends, and make an around-the-island trip.**」作者稱許對方對於入大學的憧憬及計劃，但提醒對方仍應以追求學識及建立品德為目的。

❹「**With our hearty congratulations on your splendid success, we truly hope that you'll enjoy your college life and make the best of it!**」最後再度熱忱恭賀，並以祝福對方有充實的大學生活作為結論。

英文信件 便利貼光碟 4-7 Tips：虛線是重要句型！試著模仿看看，寫信一點都不難！

A Letter of Congratulations

Dear Philip,

I was so happy to receive your letter telling us that you succeeded in getting into your ideal college. Congratulations on your dream come true!

It's a well-deserved reward for all the hard work you've done during the past three years. Your spirit and persistence in fulfilling your dream is admirable and we all share the joy and honor with you. We expect that you'll have a great college life and a promising future after graduation by either finding a good job or going on to graduate school at home or abroad.

I think it's great that you plan to join your dream student club, get to know more friends, and make an around-the-island trip. As for the part- time job you are interested in to earn college fees, I have to remind you that the pay doesn't that matter; it is safety and your attitudes that matter. Of course, mainly, you should focus on your studies and character-building, which I believe you will keep in mind as the main goals of entering college.

It's truly a big step forward to become a college student. With our hearty congratulations on your splendid success, we truly hope that you'll enjoy your college life and make the best of it!

Always affectionately,
Uncle Frank

恭賀信

親愛的菲利浦：

我很高興收到你的來信告訴我們你成功地進入你理想的大學，恭喜你夢想成真！

這是對你過去三年來付出的努力最好的獎賞。你實現夢想的精神及恆心值得讚佩，我們與你共同分享喜悅和榮耀。我們期許你將擁有美好的大學生活，畢業後，你可以找個好工作或是在國內或國外就讀研究所而創造美好的前程。

我覺得你計畫加入夢想中的社團、多認識朋友，及環島旅行是很棒的。至於你有興趣打工賺取學費的這件事，我必須要提醒你酬勞並不是那麼重要；安全和工作態度才是你應該要注意的。當然，最重要的是你必須專注於課業以及人格的建立，我相信你會謹記這一點在心並視為進入大學的主要目標。

成為大學生確實是人生的一大躍進。真誠地致上我們對你傑出成就的恭賀，我們真心期盼你將享受並善用你的大學生活！

永遠愛你的法蘭克叔叔

4-8
英文信件「邀請信」結合
「英文書信用語」句型應用
搭配文法：綜合應用句型

稱呼語（Salutation）

Dear Miss Watson:

引文與目的（Introduction and Purpose）

On behalf of our class, I'm here to send our best regards to you and sincerely invite you to our Class Reunion on 27th September. 在此謹代表我們班向您致上最誠心的問候，並且誠摯地邀請老師來參加我們九月二十七日的同學會。

內文 1（Paragraph 1）

Remembering the old senior high school days, we appreciate your being so nice to us. 回憶起往日的高中歲月，我們十分感謝老師對我們的好。

內文 2（Paragraph 2）

We really hope that you could be present, so we can bring back those happy moments we shared together. 我們非常希望老師能夠蒞臨，如此我們可以重溫往日我們共享的快樂時光。

結論與期許（Conclusion and Wishes）

Your attendance will be highly appreciated.

結尾辭與簽名（Closing and Signature）

Respectfully yours,
Simon

▶ 圖解重點說分明

關於「邀請信」的書寫

重點：撰寫邀請信應要精簡扼要，使用合宜誠懇的語氣，具體敘述舉辦的動機、時間、地點等。許久未見的師長、親友可先簡述自己的情形，接著關切對方近況，引述過去美好回憶及感恩之情，繼而提出邀請，動之以情，較易成功獲得對方樂意出席的意願。

❶「On behalf of our class, I'm here to send our best regards to you and sincerely invite you to our Class Reunion on 27th September.」引發作者撰寫此信的目的是感恩老師的辛勞，並邀請老師參加同學會。

❷「Remembering the old senior high school days, we appreciate your being so nice to us.」此部份回憶美好高中生涯的情境，強調對老師深遠的感激及謝意。

❸「We really hope that you could be present, so we can bring back those happy moments we shared together.」真誠邀約老師的蒞臨以敘舊並瞭解近況，亦可趁機向老師表達思念及感恩之情。

❹「Your attendance will be highly appreciated.」最後以誠摯的態度，期盼老師共襄盛舉，出席高中同學會作為結論。

英文信件 便利貼光碟 4-8 Tips：虛線是重要句型！試著模仿看看，寫信一點都不難！

A Letter of Invitation

Dear Miss Watson:

It is two years since our class graduated from senior high. How have you been recently? On behalf of our class, I'm here to send our best regards to you and sincerely invite you to our Class Reunion on 27th September.

We miss you a lot! Remembering the old senior high school days, we appreciate your being so nice to us. You were such a kind and responsible teacher. With your patience and guidance, we greatly progressed not only in academic performances but in personal growth. Though you had rough days dealing with our being naughty, careless, and rebellious, you never gave up on us. Under your teaching and directions, we became well-disciplined and all went to our ideal college. We cannot thank you enough!

As Teacher's Day is coming, our classmates plan the reunion party. Enclosed is the invitation card for the Class Reunion. We really hope that you could be present, so we can bring back those happy moments we shared together. And of course we will have a lot to catch up with.

Trust that you are always in the best of health and we expect your joining us in the party. <u>Your attendance will be highly appreciated.</u>

Respectfully yours,
Simon

邀請信

敬愛的華生老師：

　　我們班高中畢業迄今已過兩年了，老師近來好嗎？在此謹代表我們班向您致上最誠心的問候，並且誠摯地邀請老師來參加我們九月二十七日的同學會。

　　我們非常想念老師！回憶起往日的高中歲月，我們十分感謝老師對我們的好。您是如此仁慈又負責任的老師。有您的耐心和指導，我們不僅在課業並且在人格養成有長足的進步。雖然您在應付我們的頑皮、漫不經心，以及叛逆上嚐盡苦頭，但是您從不放棄我們。在您的教誨和指引下，我們變得有紀律，並且全都進入我們心目中理想的大學，我們非常感謝老師！

　　由於教師節即將來臨，同學們籌辦了這次的同學會，附上同學會的邀請函。我們非常希望老師能夠蒞臨，如此我們可以重溫往日我們共享的快樂時光。當然，我們還有很多新的話題可聊。

　　祝福老師永遠身體健康，並期盼您的共襄盛舉。我們將會十分感謝老師的蒞臨。

敬愛您的賽門

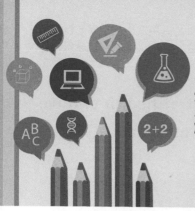

4-9

英文信件「寫給外國筆友的信」結合「英文書信用語」句型應用

搭配文法：綜合應用句型

▶ **圖解寫作架構**

稱呼語（Salutation）

Dear Jeff,

引文與目的（Introduction and Purpose）

And now, I am free to plan for the coming summer vacation we're going to spend together. 現在我有空來規劃我們即將共度的暑假。

內文 1（Paragraph 1）

You just couldn't miss the two places here! 你絕對不能錯過這兩個地方！

內文 2（Paragraph 2）

You would love them a lot and you can eat to your heart's content. 你一定會很喜愛這些美食，而且你可以盡情地吃。

結論與期許（Conclusion and Wishes）

With my help, I hope you can fully enjoy the beauty of Taiwan. 經由我的導覽，我希望你可以充分享受台灣之美。

結尾辭與簽名（Closing and Signature）

Sincerely yours,
Linda

圖解重點說分明

關於「寫給外國筆友的信」的書寫

重點：寫給外國筆友的信時，語氣可輕鬆自在，熱列慇勤。大致説明自己的近況，並關心對方。描述預定引導外國筆友遊臺灣的具體計畫外，更要強調預定遊覽處各自獨有的特色，主動積極，展現歡迎筆友的用心及熱忱，藉以加深筆友的印象及前來遊玩的意願。

❶「**And now, I am free to plan for the coming summer vacation we're going to spend together.**」説明作者先前忙期末考，未能及時回信的歉意及此時預擬與筆友同遊台灣的計畫。

❷「**You just couldn't miss the two places here!**」此部份介紹外國筆友必遊的兩個景點及其特色。

❸「**You would love them a lot and you can eat to your heart's content.**」此部份強調另外兩個必遊的景點及其特色供外國筆友瞭解。

❹「**With my help, I hope you can fully enjoy the beauty of Taiwan.**」最後以熱忱的態度，表達期盼外國筆友早日來訪的心願作為結論。

英文信件 便利貼光碟 4-9 Tips：虛線是重要句型！試著模仿看看，寫信一點都不難！

A Letter to a Foreign Pen Pal

Dear Jeff,

Sorry that I didn't answer your letter sooner, as I was busy preparing for the final exams before school ended. And now, I am free to plan for the coming summer vacation we're going to spend together.

I'm so excited and happy about your visiting Taiwan soon. As soon as you arrive, the first place I'll show you is the tallest building in Taiwan, the famous Taipei 101. Another great place to visit is the National Palace Museum. It is well-known for its largest collection of Chinese paintings and artifacts in the world. You just couldn't miss the two places here!

The next scenic spot I'd like to show you around is Kenting, where there're the most beautiful beaches and scenery for us to enjoy. And finally, we must experience the unique feature of Taiwan, the night markets. Most night markets in Taiwan have their own local features. The food at the stalls may vary greatly from traditional Chinese delicacies to authentic Taiwanese snacks. You would love them a lot and you can eat to your heart's content.

It's a pity that you cannot stay here for long. <u>With my help,
I hope you can fully enjoy the beauty of Taiwan.</u> Look forward
to seeing you soon.

Sincerely yours,
Linda

寫給外國筆友的信

親愛的傑夫：

很抱歉我沒有早點回信，因為當時我正忙於準備學校結束前的期末考試。現在我有空來規劃我們即將共度的暑假。

對於你即將來台灣，我感到很興奮及開心。你一抵達，第一個我將帶你去參觀的是台灣最高的建築物，著名的台北 101。另一個我們要去參觀的很棒的地方是故宮博物院。它是以擁有全世界數量最多的中國繪畫以及手工製品而著名。你絕對不能錯過這兩個地方！

下一個我打算帶你去觀光的景點是墾丁，這裡擁有最美麗的海灘和風景供我們欣賞。最後，我們一定要體驗台灣獨有的特色，夜市。台灣大部分的夜市有它們自己的地方色彩。食物攤販所販售的食物包羅萬象，從傳統的中國菜餚到道地的台灣小吃都有，你一定會很喜愛這些美食，而且你可以盡情地吃。

很可惜的是你不能在台灣久待，經由我的導覽，我希望你可以充分享受台灣之美。期盼早日見面。

您最誠摯的琳達

4-10

英文信件結合英文書信用語
句型應用小練習

▶ 英文信件結合英文書信用語句型小回顧

　　「英文信件」就格式而言，主要是由下列常見的七個部份組成的：

1. 信頭（Heading）：寄信人地址與寄信日期。

2. 稱呼語（Salutation）：Dear＋稱呼用詞，後方一般接逗點，正式信件則接冒號。

3. 正文（Body）：包含有引文（Greeting or Introduction）、主體（Main Paragraphs）、與結尾（Conclusion）。

4. 結尾敬辭（Closing）：如 Truly yours 第一個字字首大寫，最後加逗點。

5. 簽名（Signature）：名字簽在結尾敬辭的下面、中間的地方。

6. 附筆（Postscript/PS）：以簡短一個句子附加要補充或遺漏的事項。

7. 附件（Enclosure）：寫明所寄文件的內容（兩件以上可寫明件數）。

　　英文信件一般依照上述格式書寫，內容則會依信件的目的及動機而有所不同。

▶ 文法句型補一補

( ) 1. Miss Banks was ＿＿＿＿ angry that she demanded an apology.

(A) so   (B) as   (C) such   (D) too

( ) 2. ＿＿＿＿ was Mr. White that asked for an early morning call.

(A) As   (B) This   (C) It   (D) There

( ) 3. House prices went up high; ＿＿＿＿, average salary remained low.

(A) and thus   (B) but

(C) by contrast   (D) contrary

( ) 4. ＿＿＿＿ you decide to hire me or not, I appreciate your time and consideration.

(A) What   (B) Whether   (C) Which   (D) where

( ) 5. ＿＿＿＿ you aren't satisfied with our products, I wish to make some compensation.

(A) If   (B) Such   (C) Provide   (D) After

( ) 6. Monica ＿＿＿＿ a lot of time upgrading the product into a more popular style.

(A) paid   (B) cost   (C) took   (D) spent

1. (A) so

題目中譯 班克斯小姐是如此地生氣以至於她要求對方要道歉。

答案解析 so … that … 表示「如此地……以至於……」，後接子句是表示「結果」的固定句型。故應選 (A) so。

2. (C) It

題目中譯 是懷特先生要求一大清早的催醒電話。

答案解析 「分裂句」句型：It is/was … that …（是～才是～）用以強調訊息焦點。故應選 (C) It。

3. (C) by contrast

題目中譯 房價高漲；相較之下，平均薪資仍舊很低。

答案解析 by contrast 是表示相反、對照的片語。此句是兩個前後語意相反成對比的子句故應要選 (C) by contrast。

4. (B) Whether

題目中譯 無論你是否決定要僱用我，我都感謝您花費的時間及考慮。

答案解析 Whether＋子句＋or not，主詞＋動詞……（無論是～或不是，……。）是表示讓步的固定句型。故選 (B) Whether。

5. (A) If

題目中譯 假使您對我們的產品不滿意，我希望能做補償。

答案解析 由後半段得知是假設語氣的語意及用法，故答案應選 (A) If。

6. (D) spent

題目中譯 莫妮卡花很多時間讓她的產品升級成為更受歡迎的款式。

答案解析 特殊動詞 spend 的用法：某人花時間或花錢用 spend，接動名詞。故應選 (D) spent。

▶ 寫作老師巧巧說

　　如同一般英文文章寫作一樣，撰寫「英文信件」時，除了注意正確的書信格式外，要有開頭段、內容主體可有二或三個段落，及結論段。寫作原則方面要能簡潔明瞭，語氣誠懇中肯，內容確實完整，並且自然口語化。可依不同主題，如求職應徵、查詢、請求、抱怨、感謝、恭賀、邀請、給筆友的信，……等等，活用各種相關的文法及句型，即可寫出成功合宜的英文信。

文法/生活英語 **002**

圖解式英文句型＋作文：Basic（附便利貼光碟）

作　　　者	孟瑞秋
發 行 人	周瑞德
執行總監	齊心瑀
業務經理	楊景輝
企劃編輯	饒美君
校　　對	編輯部
封面構成	高鍾琪

內頁構成	菩薩蠻數位文化有限公司
印　　製	大亞彩色印刷製版股份有限公司
初　　版	2017 年 5 月
定　　價	新台幣 379 元
出　　版	倍斯特出版事業有限公司
電　　話	(02) 2351-2007
傳　　真	(02) 2351-0887
地　　址	100 台北市中正區福州街 1 號 10 樓之 2
E - m a i l	best.books.service@gmail.com
網　　址	www.bestbookstw.com

港澳地區總經銷	泛華發行代理有限公司
地　　　　址	香港新界將軍澳工業邨駿昌街 7 號 2 樓
電　　　　話	(852) 2798-2323
傳　　　　真	(852) 2796-5471

國家圖書館出版品預行編目資料

圖解式英文句型＋作文. Basic / 孟瑞秋
著. -- 初版. -- 臺北市 ：倍斯特,
2017.05 面；　公分. --（文法/生活英
語 002）
ISBN 978-986-94428-4-8(平裝附光碟片)
1. 英語 2. 寫作法
　　805.17　　　　　　　106004756

Simply Learning, Simply Best

Simply Learning, Simply Best